Also By Wendy J. Hatfield
Beyond The Cedar Gate
Elizabeth and The Savages UnChained

Also By Cendy J. Hatfield
CHEDDERVILLE TAILS
THE LEGEND OF LIMBERGER FOREST

NOVELETTES
From
Elizabeth and The Savages UnChained

Wendy J. Hatfield
Cendy J. Hatfield

Edited By: Goldie Carlon

authorHOUSE

AuthorHouse™
1663 Liberty Drive
Bloomington, IN 47403
www.authorhouse.com
Phone: 833-262-8899

© 2023 Wendy J. Hatfield, Cendy J. Hatfield. All rights reserved.

No part of this book may be reproduced, stored in a retrieval system, or transmitted by any means without the written permission of the author.

Published by AuthorHouse 06/02/2023

ISBN: 979-8-8230-0565-4 (sc)
ISBN: 979-8-8230-0563-0 (hc)
ISBN: 979-8-8230-0564-7 (e)

Library of Congress Control Number: 2023906543

Print information available on the last page.

A few lines from the poem, "The Last Rose of Summer", written by Thomas Moore is featured on this book.
Moore, Thomas. "The Last Rose of Summer" 1805. American Literature. https://americanliterature.com/author/thomas-moore/poem/the-last-rose-of-summer

This book is printed on acid-free paper.

Because of the dynamic nature of the Internet, any web addresses or links contained in this book may have changed since publication and may no longer be valid. The views expressed in this work are solely those of the author and do not necessarily reflect the views of the publisher, and the publisher hereby disclaims any responsibility for them.

Contents

Deep Dark Secrets
Written By:
Wendy J. Hatfield
Cendy J. Hatfield

Prologue 3
Chapter 1 5
Chapter 2 11
Chapter 3 15
Chapter 4 17

Buckles O'Leary
Written By:
Wendy J. Hatfield
Cendy J. Hatfield

Chapter 1 25
Chapter 2 33
Chapter 3 39
Chapter 4 49

Dance of The Sugar Plum Wienie
Written By:
Cendy J. Hatfield

Chapter 1 61
Chapter 2 71
Chapter 3 81

Albert and The Glass Figurine
Written By:
Wendy J. Hatfield

Chapter 1	97
Chapter 2	105
Chapter 3	117

Brave are those who are sure of defeat,
yet they do not leave the field.
-Unknown

Deep Dark Secrets

Written By:

Wendy J. Hatfield
Cendy J. Hatfield

Prologue

I have a story to tell you, and it's not for the faint of heart. It's a story of jealousy, deception, and deep dark secrets. A story like mine should never be spoken of when any one puppy is alone and never ever in the dark. But, before we begin, I should tell you about me and my siblings.

I was 6 months old, just a puppy and the newest member of my family, and my new sister Sager Jane was not happy about it at all. Then there is my brother Mr. Wienie; what can I say about him. Just listen to my story, and then you can decide.

Let me start with Sager. She takes forever when she eats because my sister eats one bite at a time. She seems to think that if she eats one bite at a time, chewing every bite ten times, she will stay thin, but hello, she's chunky. Oops! Please don't tell Sager I said that.

Then there's my brother; he never takes very long to eat. Sometimes when Mr. Wienie teases me too much, I like to call him Mr. Piglet under my breath because he eats super-fast. When he's finished eating, he gets what Grandma calls the wind from not chewing his food very well. Grandma tells my brother the wind is his superpower! I'm not sure how something so smelly is a superpower, but it must be because Grandma says so! I think we should just call him Mr. Stinky Bottom, but don't tell my brother I say that.

I was still trying to get to know my family better because I could tell they weren't sure if they liked me yet. Mr. Wienie would play with me, but only if Sager was asleep. I knew Sager was upset because she wasn't the baby anymore; I was, and she made it known. Sager treated me like an outsider and never let me play with her when she was playing until that one morning in the yard when Sager said I was about to meet my destiny.

Chapter 1

THAT MORNING WE RACED THROUGH THE HOUSE TO the front door, where we lined up, waiting for the door to be opened. Racing out to the grass, I heard Mommy say, "There goes my herd of rabid savages." Then she went back into the house, laughing as she went. We ran to Grandma's dogwood tree in the yard. I love it there; the tree has pretty little pink flowers. I think all the birds must think so too. They like to hang out on a small box with a hole in it stuck on a branch in the tree. Sager calls it the giving tree. I'm not sure yet what it gives, but I bet it must be something special. Maybe it's because mommy gives it birdseed and corn every day.

It was terrific when we all lept from the porch, and there was still dew in the grass. I could feel the warmth from the early morning sun on my back, and the urge to take the lead was almost too much to hold back, but I held back anyway. I was so excited that I couldn't stand myself; because during breakfast that day, Mr. Wienie told me they would show me a secret in the yard.

They had finally invited me to play. Sager said I could very well meet my destiny this morning. I didn't know what a destiny was or what secrets are, but I'm just happy Sager wants me to join in the fun. I felt hopeful that maybe this day was the day I would be part of the family instead of the one who took Sager's spot as the baby.

A short couple of bounds later, we stood under the tree. Sager picked up a stick, laid down, and started chewing on it as I watched Mr. Wienie running around the tree's trunk, nosing the ground. I waited impatiently for my brother to tell me the secret.

Scanning the yard, wondering where my destiny was, I locked eyes with Sager. I hadn't realized she was staring at me; it made me feel nervous. She lay there chewing at the bark of the stick, staring at me. I could tell she was sizing me up like she always does. She asked me, "Do you know what a secret is, Elizabeth?" Before I could answer her, she asked me another question, "Elizabeth, did you know that rabbits keep secrets?"

Mr. Wienie continued to nose the ground, pausing every so often to glance around the yard while Sager questioned me. Sager's eyes became huge as she barked, "Deep dark secrets, Elizabeth."

Mr. Wienie lifted his head and said, "Yes, deep dark secrets. Rabbits keep them."

I thought, oh my gosh, deep dark secrets. Would mommy approve of these secrets? My mind raced as I thought, am I ready for this?

Sager looked at Mr. Wienie and stated, "I bet Elizabeth can't even keep a secret."

Sager had asked so many questions at one time she had not given me a chance to answer, and before I could stop myself, I barked back at her, "I can too! I can keep a secret! Tell me what a secret is, then I can keep it!" Sager looked at me and asked, "Do you know how hard it is to get a rabbit to give up its secrets?"

Mr. Wienie interrupted, telling Sager, "We need to tell Elizabeth about the secrets of the rabbits before we show her. She needs to understand that rabbits have secrets, deep dark secrets." Sniffing the air, he said, "Listen." Then turning his head, pointing with his nose, he whispered, "Look, it's the rabbit; he is across the yard over there. Be still, or he will run away."

Sager patted the ground; she wanted me to lay down beside her so Mr. Wienie could tell me about the rabbits and the kind of secrets they kept. A shiver of excitement went through me. I was going to find out what rabbits were and how to get them to give up their secrets.

As though pausing for dramatic effect, Mr. Wienie lowered his voice, saying, "Long ago in this very yard on a morning much like this one, Sager and I went on walkabout, and a stone rabbit appeared out of nowhere." Mr. Wienie lowered his voice to just above a whisper, pointed, and said, "The very one that is standing in our yard right now. Elizabeth, that one. That rabbit stood so still and quiet. Sager and I think that's why he turned to stone."

Gasping, I dared to look in the direction that my brother pointed. How many times had I been past this rabbit? I never really paid attention to that part of the yard before. Mr. Wienie looked over his shoulder; when he looked back, his eyes became more serious. He moved closer in the grass, right in front of us, and again barely above a whisper, he said, "Late at night, you can hear the sounds of the rabbit gnawing on his food."

Sager stood up and gnawed viciously at the stick she had been chewing on. She was pretending to be the rabbit gnawing on its food. Suddenly she stopped; her eyes were big, pretending to pull on something heavy. She said, "Wienie, don't forget, you can hear the rabbit's feet on the walkway late at night while he drags that heavy bucket." She looked right into my eyes, and I felt terrified; I was afraid of what I would hear Mr. Wienie say next. I was young and gullible back then.

Mr. Wienie continued, "The rabbit is as quiet as the wind, and he can move within the shadows of the full noonday."

"Elizabeth, the secrets are in the bucket!" Sager said, laying back down beside me. "But wait," she added, "that's not all that is in the bucket Elizabeth."

I knew my eyes were huge, but I couldn't help it and tried not to sound afraid when I asked my sister what else was in the bucket. That's when Sager held up her paw, sounding worried, and said, "Mom will be mad if we scare her, Wienie. Elizabeth is too much of a puppy to hear the rest of the story."

I shook my head no and told Sager I wasn't afraid. I wanted them to accept me and treat me like their sister. Sager looked at Mr. Wienie and said, "Elizabeth must take the oath before we go any farther. She has seen too much and now knows about the rabbit's bucket. Elizabeth has to abide by the codes of the yard before meeting her destiny. It's time, Wienie; she has come too far to turn back now."

Oh my gosh, I thought, what could be in the bucket besides secrets? What are the codes of the yard? I wondered if it was something to eat, Mr. Wienie eats all the time. Maybe that's what it is. It's food.

Then Mommy yelled from the porch. "Num, nums who wants a num num?"

Mr. Wienie charged off. Sager jumped up, stretched her back, and said, "Come on pup, mom's calling; the codes and everything else can wait until tomorrow."

When I reached the porch, mommy picked me up and asked if I was having fun. Yes, mommy. I thought, licking her face in response.

I shivered in delight, knowing that on this day, I almost came face to face with my destiny as Sager said I would! Almost!

I still have no idea what secrets are and how to keep them, and as for this destiny thing, it will have to wait until tomorrow; I bet it's going to be the best day ever! But the most wonderful part of the morning was that Sager treated me like a sister and didn't send me away.

Chapter 2

THE FOLLOWING MORNING, WE HAD BREAKFAST, AND mommy let us out the front door. Sager was first, then me, and then Mr. Wienie. This made me feel like I was growing up, especially after almost meeting with my destiny face-to-face yesterday by the giving tree.

Sager called over her shoulder as she led the way down the steps into the yard, "Today is the day mom gives the giving tree corn and seeds. She puts it in the little house that hangs from one of the bottom limbs. As soon as she finishes and goes back in the house, Mr. Wienie will call our meeting to order in the clubhouse."

I thought, oh, what a magical day as I ran past Sager, making it around the tree trunk first. Mr. Wienie was close behind Sager as we all lined up to wait for mommy to cross the yard with her tins full of grain and seeds.

Mr. Wienie nosed around the tree's base, looking for bacon bits, as he called it. Sager rolled over on her back next to me and started to itch around in the grass. I played at trying to catch the end of her tail; side note for you young pups; don't ever try to catch your big sister's tail. It's awkward and never ends well. No matter how fun it might look, Sager will tell you that this is why every puppy is born with its own tail.

Sager sat up from wiggling in the wet grass and asked Mr. Wienie, "Why do you always think you are going to find bacon bits and a river of gravy?"

Throwing himself down next to Sager, Mr. Wienie said, "You know, like the song mom sings to me, I wish were an oscar meyer wienie, although I am not exactly who this oscar meyer person is that she speaks of. But I love the thoughts of a gravy river with bacon bits to float downstream on."

Sager and Mr. Wienie lay on their backs, looking up at mommy, then the most beautiful thing happened. Mommy bent down and rubbed Sager and Mr. Wienie's bellies. I jumped from my place beside Sager and leaned against mommy's legs, and she rubbed my belly too.

As mommy walked back to the porch, Mr. Wienie cleared his throat and, in a very official voice, said, "I now call this day to order, Sager, Master of Arms! Elizabeth, Private Pledge, proceed to the clubhouse."

As Sager and I lined up to march to the clubhouse behind Mr. Wienie, he called out, "For all the cheerios in Grandma's cereal bowl, one, two, one, two!"

"Quickly, Elizabeth, run to the clubhouse," Sager said, giggling as she nipped me and ran at Mr. Wienie's heels.

So, there I was, standing in front of the clubhouse doors. It was finally going to happen. They were going to let me into the club; I was about to be one of them. Sager told me many times before today that I just wasn't old enough to know the yard codes yet.

Mr. Wienie started the official entry dance. He cleared his throat, and in his best singing voice, he sang, "You put your right paw in, you pull your left paw out, then you shake your butt all around. You do the." Mr. Wienie stopped and asked, "Am I doing this right, Sager?"

Watching Mr. Wienie's silly two-legged dance, I thought, gosh, this is all so complicated. How will I ever remember this dance and the song, and only on two legs?

Becoming irritated, Sager pushed past Mr. Wienie, saying, "You're cutting into my naptime here in the clubhouse."

As I followed Sager into the hedge, I opened my eyes wide. I wanted to take it all in at once. Making this moment of being accepted a long memory, I would never forget. Trying to remember all the smells and all the songs around me. I sat poised, quivering with excitement.

Then all of a sudden, we heard it! Mr. Wienie farted as he squeezed past me to what he called his podium. The smell was more than we could handle. Sager covered her nose, and I fanned the air with my tail.

Sniffing and looking around, trying to blame his mistake on anything other than himself, Mr. Wienie said, "I now call this counsel of rabid savages to order. Sager, Master of Arms, prepare to speak the codes of the yard, and Elizabeth, Private Pledge, prepare to repeat the codes!"

I thought to myself, finally, we are getting to the codes. In a very official voice, Mr. Wienie recited the codes, "Code number one: I swear never to poop in or around the walkways. Code number two: I vow never to dig in mom's flower beds. Code number three: I swear to protect and make as much noise as possible when the mailman comes." Snickering, he added, "Code number four: I will give Mr. Wienie all of my treats for a week!"

Sager and I started to repeat the codes; she stopped, looked up at Mr. Wienie, and barked. "Don't you dare, Wienie! Why is everything always about your stomach? Must I remind you of the smell you graced us with as you squeezed through the clubhouse door a few minutes ago?"

Sager and Mr. Wienie discussed the codes, going back and forth over who was right and who wasn't. I could hear mommy on the pathway, so I peeked outside of the clubhouse. She was digging in the rabbit's bucket.

I darted out of the clubhouse, making mommy look up, and she called to us, saying, "Time for treats."

I ran to mommy, and as she picked me up, I got a quick glance into the rabbit's bucket. I saw white flowers with juicy-looking red berries in it. I wondered if those were the rabbit's secrets and how many were in there? It had been such a glorious morning. Sager and Mr. Wienie filed into the house while mommy carried me behind them. She asked, "What have you been up to, young lady?" I just laid back in her arms and let her rub my belly. I moved to lick her face, and that's when I swear I saw the rabbit move.

"Sager, Mr. Wienie, come back. Hurry, it's the rabbit; he's going to gnaw on some poor vegetable!" I yelled and barked while trying to wiggle out of mommy's arms as she closed the front door. She kissed my forehead and put me on the floor. "Who wants a treat?" She asked as she headed to the kitchen.

Chapter 3

THE RABBIT WOULD HAVE TO WAIT. SAGER AND MR. Wienie had already raced to the kitchen and were waiting. Barking and jumping up and down with excitement, I followed mommy and forgot all about the rabbit. She grabbed our treat bag, and that's when I noticed that some of the treats in the bag looked just like the juicy red berries I had just seen in the rabbit's bucket. Suddenly my thoughts flew back to the bucket. I knew right then and there that the rabbit had stolen our treats. Oh, my goodness, I thought; the juicy treats my siblings, and I were chewing on suddenly tasted like secrets. I barked and ran to the door, barking again, yelling, "I think I know your secret, rabbit, white and red secrets."

Hoping this could be the secret, I barked again in excited anticipation. Sager had almost finished her treat when I returned to the kitchen. I hurried and finished mine. It was delicious. Mr. Wienie licked his lips, and I licked his face, too; we all laughed, racing to the front door. When mommy opened the door, Mr. Wienie was in the lead. Sager said we needed to meet at the giving tree after our walkabout.

Walkabout, this is when I will get to sneak a peek into that rabbit's bucket. I thought I would walk up to that rabbit and tell him; I saw you move.

Then I quivered with anticipation. I wasn't going to tell Sager and Mr, Wienie what I saw in the rabbit's bucket earlier when mommy picked me up. But I was too excited and couldn't help myself. I jumped up and down beside Sager, yelling, telling her what I had seen earlier. But all she did was sniff her way behind Mr. Wienie to the middle of the yard; I could tell they didn't believe me. I panicked and blurted out my plans to peek into the rabbit's bucket. Both Sager and Mr. Wienie stopped walking. Mr. Wienie turned his head to look at Sager, then at the bucket. His eyes darted back and forth at the rabbit, then to his huge bucket of red and white secrets. With a commanding voice, he said, "Sager, Master of Arms! Elizabeth, Sergeant of Airs! As soon as the mailman walks by the yard, meet me at the giving tree."

Sager returned to sniffing the ground; she was waiting for the mailman. She could see that he was still three or four houses away, but he would be walking by any minute. She told me to get any unfinished business done and to be ready for him. I was still confused about who this Sergeant of Airs was and where he was hiding. She must have seen the confusion on my face and told me the best news I had ever heard; in fact, it's what spurred me to throw my heart into the codes of the yard. She said, "My silly sister, you are Sergeant of Airs. Our brother has given you your official yard name. As soon as we finish with code number three, we will meet back at the giving tree and have your official naming ceremony."

Chapter 4

EXHAUSTED FROM BARKING AT THE MAILMAN, I THREW myself on the grass at the giving tree. Feeling sleepy, I started drifting off, and suddenly, I remembered the rabbit's bucket. Jumping to my feet, I tried to tell Sager and Mr. Wienie again that I had seen the rabbit move. They both spun around to look at me, then looked at each other. Out of the corner of my eye, I saw Mr. Wienie wink at Sager. She had a little twinkle in her eye.

Before I could tell them what I saw, Mr. Wienie interrupted, saying, "It's time for the naming ceremony. Sager, Master of Arms, Elizabeth is no longer a private. She will be known as Elizabeth, Sergeant of Airs. This is how Elizabeth will be addressed from now on inside and outside of the clubhouse. Now line up and make ready to march."

Mr. Wienie began to march in place. He called out, "It is going to be blistering hot on our way to the clubhouse, but march, we must for all the toasted cheese sandwiches mommy makes, one, two and a one, two now march!"

We were on our way to the clubhouse. I felt excited and couldn't wait to finish telling them how I had seen the rabbit move. We all did the two-legged dance and entered the clubhouse. I was so nervous and surprised that I remembered the song and the dance. I wanted to scream when Mr. Wienie said we needed to recite the codes of the yard again. I had seen the rabbit move, and there was no time for reciting the codes. As we finished the codes, we all repeated that if we ever break a yard code, may our flea medicine never work again.

Winking at Sager, Mr. Wienie cleared his throat and said, "Master of Arms, it has been brought to my attention that our sister, I mean Elizabeth, I mean Sergeant of Airs, has seen the rabbit move."

I was so excited I blurted out, "I did... I saw him move while mommy was...." Mr. Wienie held up his paw and interrupted me, asking Sager if she thought I was ready to take on a secret mission of recon involving the rabbit's bucket.

Sager replied, "Yes, I think she can do it, Colonel." I shivered with excitement. My brother and sister thought I could do it, but I wasn't sure what they were talking about.

I listened to Mr. Wienie's plan; he said, "Okay, now hear this, Sergeant of Airs; as we leave the clubhouse, you slowly walk toward the rabbit. Remember, don't make any sudden moves, and don't walk too fast just yet. Master of Arms will fake an injury, and I will call mom to the door. As soon as the door opens, you can run and jump into the rabbit's bucket."

Sager kissed my forehead, saying, "It is going to be hard, Sergeant of Airs, but we know you can do it." We started to get into our positions when Mr. Wienie stopped and said, "Oh, one more thing! Look for the color red." He licked his lips and said, "That will be the secrets you are looking for! They need to be delivered to my bed for further inspection."

So, there I was on my first recon mission, strolling slowly along the walkway toward the rabbit and his bucket. Nervously I kept repeating what the Colonel had said; he said be brave, and he said something about red. Oh, I thought to myself, what was I supposed to do with the red?

As Sager and Mr. Wienie were turning to climb the front steps, I followed the walkway. I approached the rabbit's bucket and stopped right in front of it. I looked all around me, and with a rush of adrenaline, I shouted, "Okay, I'm here!"

I was shaking, still trying to remember what the Colonel said about the red. I felt deep in my heart that mommy would not like these spoils of war. He and Master of Arms started barking to get mommy's attention. That's when I felt my new yard name come into play. It was glorious; my ears floated on the wind when I leaped through the air into the rabbit's bucket. I could see Sager and Mr. Wienie for a brief moment standing on the porch. I landed perfectly. The first thing I noticed was the sweet smell of dirt. Sniffing, I walked carefully around the inside of this unknown world, then I saw it!

The white and red secrets. Lots of red hanging from green leafy branches. There were hundreds of red secrets everywhere. This bucket was full.

Calming myself, I remembered Mr. Wienie saying, 'Bring the red.' So, I closed my eyes and snapped off the branch that held the red secrets. Then with all my might, I leaped to safety. As soon as my feet hit the walkway, I was running. I ran so fast I had to jump over Sager and Mr. Wienie, who were blocking the doorway, keeping mommy busy with Sager's supposedly hurt foot. I kept my head down, so mommy wouldn't see that I had the secrets in my mouth. Sager winked at me as I sailed through the air into the house. I headed toward Mr. Wienie's bed. This was all part of his war plan; it worked like a charm, just as the Colonel said it would. I stashed the secrets in the blankets of Mr. Wienie's bed and waited.

Mommy picked Sager up; I could hear her whining as mommy carried her into the house. It seemed like an hour before Sager, and Mr. Wienie came running into the room. Sager said, "I'm not playing the wounded pup in your spoils of war plan anymore, Wienie. Mommy almost called the doctor."

"But Sager, you're such a good actress." He replied.

As Sager and Mr. Wienie argued, I dug into the blankets and pulled out the secrets. Mr. Wienie said, "I get first dibs," and Sager said, "OH, NO, YOU DON'T, WIENIE!"

"Present the secrets, and do not hold back!" Mr. Wienie barked, then continued, "There had better be red on them."

As I presented the secrets, it became an all-out tussle. Suddenly, I heard mommy coming. She was calling for us when she came through the door. She sucked in her breath and exclaimed, "You little savages, you got into the strawberries! Look at the mess you made of yourselves and Mr. Wienie's bed!"

Mr. Wienie cried out, "It wasn't me, mommy."

Sager whined, "It was Mr. Stinky Butt's plan. I didn't want to do it. Wienie said if we sent Elizabeth to get the strawberries, we wouldn't get in trouble cause she's the baby. We were only playing a trick on her. Wienie needs to be in trouble, not me."

Mommy picked me up, cuddled me in her arms, and sang as she washed my face. I sighed contentedly, they tried to play a trick on me, but I always knew what strawberries were. I did not want to break their hearts, and I played along every step of the way. This was the day that my sister and brother each unknowingly referred to me as their sister. Right then and there, I knew that my new brother and sister loved and accepted me as much as my mommy did, and I loved them too.

The End

Buckles O'Leary

Written By:

Wendy J. Hatfield
Cendy J. Hatfield

Chapter 1

IT WAS THREE IN THE MORNING, AND VISIONS OF BACON were dancing in my head. It was terrific; I could smell it and almost taste it. I was dreaming that my mom was standing at the stove frying bacon. She told me that as long as I cleaned my plate, she would make me as much bacon as I could eat. Mom had the bacon in her hand; it glistened and smelled heavenly. As she leaned over to put it in my bowl, I licked my lips in preparation to have a bite. At that moment, I heard something, and it woke me up. I squeezed my eyes shut as I rolled over and tried to return to my dream. But now, I was wide awake. What could this noise be that has woken me from the dream of my dreams? With my eyes open, I lay there listening for a minute; I heard it again. I sat up to look around, but nothing was there.

I went to the kitchen to get a drink of water and heard the noise again as I left Grandma's room. I ran as fast as possible, barking all the way; I hoped it was mom serving breakfast early, and I wanted her to know I was ready to eat! I was positive I heard the noise coming from the kitchen. Excited, I rounded the corner into the kitchen from the hallway, and with a few short leaps and bounds, I was in front of my bowl. The kitchen was dark, and my bowl was empty. Mom was nowhere to be found. I was just hearing things, I thought to myself.

Beguiled and disappointed, I went to mom's room to check on my sisters, Sager Jane, and Elizabeth. Sager was muttering in her sleep; she said something about her boyfriends, the Jersey Beach Boys, and being hungry. I returned to Grandma's room. I heard the same noise again when I jumped on the couch to arrange my blankets. As I turned to look in the direction of the noise, I saw the drawer in Grandma's end table begin to open. I froze with excitement; Grandma keeps her snacks in there. I once found a ham sandwich with mayo and tomatoes; it was a delicious find that day!

Excited, I forgot all about the noise I had just heard. I hurried to the drawer, thinking it would be great to have an early morning snack to start my day. I peeked into the drawer that was now halfway open, and that's when it happened; a tiny man dressed in green with a top hat was standing in Grandma's drawer. He was holding an empty black pot and appeared to be searching for something.

Shocked, I resisted the urge to bark. We were face to face now, and the little man froze midstep. He then stepped back and bowed to me. I sniffed the air, unsure if I should trust this little man dressed all in green. Wondering why he was in Grandma's drawer and worried if he had eaten all the snacks. The little man began to dance. He sang a song about a pot of gold at the end of the rainbow and something about needing his hat back. Holding up my paw, I interrupted and asked him, "Where are my Grandma's snacks?"

He answered, "Where are the snacks, asks you? They are with my treasures, says I." I tilted my head to the side as I listened to his voice. He had a strange accent as he sang his words; they all seemed to spin in circles.

I could hear Sager barking; I looked over my shoulder to see if she was coming down the hallway. When I looked back to the drawer, the little man was gone but had left his black pot behind. I climbed into the drawer to see if he was hiding. I called out to him, saying, "Little man, where did you go? Hello, are you there? Where are the snacks? You forgot your black pot."

"Mr. Wienie, who are you talking to?" I heard Sager say, causing me to bump my head in the drawer as I backed out. I was surprised my sister hadn't questioned me more as I followed her back to the kitchen. Since she had been on a diet, I could tell Sager was eager for breakfast.

For the last couple of months, my sisters, Sager and Elizabeth, have been boy-crazy; all they think and talk about are boys and clothes. Get this, Elizabeth's boyfriend is a guitar-playing Prince from Italy, and his name is Elvis. Elizabeth and Elvis write letters back and forth at least once a week. Elvis wrote Elizabeth, saying he and his family would soon be moving to the United States.

Sager recently started dating twin boys from New Jersey. She calls them the Jersey Beach Boys. Yesterday, Sager received a package in the mail containing a pearl necklace along with a letter from the twins asking her to be their queen. Oh my god, let's not forget about Snoopy! Snoopy is Sager's lifelong crush. Every day since she was a young pup, she has written a letter to Snoopy, hoping he would come to visit her. It's been over five years, and Snoopy still hasn't shown up. But that's a story for another time.

My sisters and I lined up, waiting for our bowls to be filled. Sitting in front of my bowl, I was still thinking about that little man dressed all in green. I wondered how he got into our house and how long had he been hiding in Grandma's snack drawer. I felt nervous not knowing how many of Grandma's snacks he has managed to eat without me knowing about it. Mom filled our bowls. Sager and Elizabeth started to eat, but I could only sit there trying to recall the song that the little man had sung to me.

Elizabeth stopped eating, raising her head from her bowl; she swallowed, asking me, "Are you alright, brother? Why aren't you chowing down on your food?" I looked at her and then at Sager; I wanted to tell them about the little man I found in Grandma's snack drawer. Instead, I told them about my dream of the endless supply of bacon mom was going to make for me. Sager swallowed hard, saying, "Not now, Mr. Wienie; I'm super hungry; this diet I've been on is starving me to death."

"But it's worth it, Sager! Your new dress is going to look amazing on you." Elizabeth said before diving into her bowl to have another bite. Sager nodded yes as she took another bite; talking with her mouth full, she said, "Those Jersey Beach Boys are good-looking, and I love the necklace they sent me."

"Snoopy will be so jealous when and if he ever gets here." Elizabeth said playfully, teasing Sager. They both looked at each other, laughed, and continued to eat while Elizabeth talked about her recent letter from Prince Elvis.

Mom returned to the room, asking, "Who wants to go outside?" I quickly ate my food and followed my mom and sisters to the front door. While mom held the door open, telling us to behave, we raced off the porch, running to the tree in our front yard.

Buckles O'Leary

While Sager nosed the ground, she asked me what I was doing this morning with my head in Grandma's snack drawer. I explained what happened in Grandma's room with the little man dressed all in green. I replied that I needed her and Elizabeth's help to find this little guy. Sager sat down and stared at me as if she had never seen me before, "This sounds like a made-up story, Wienie; I need to know what you are up to right now." Sager demanded. Elizabeth interrupted Sager telling me, "I'm not falling for your tricks again, Wienie. Don't even try to get half of my snacks ever again." Elizabeth ranted, reminding me about all the times I had played tricks on her.

It's true; I had tricked Elizabeth with harmless made-up stories to get her snacks in the past. But this time, I was being serious; I knew I wasn't dreaming. I saw a little man dressed in green. He spoke to me, and I was sure his black pot was still in Grandma's snack drawer.

Sager interrupted, laughing; she said, "No, Elizabeth, that's not how it's going to work this time, Wienie needs our help, so he has to share his treats with us." I promised Sager I would give her my whole dinner if she just looked in the drawer and let me show her the black pot the little man left behind.

Elizabeth stood in front of Sager, pleading with her not to take my food. She said, "You have three pounds to lose, and you're halfway there. Your dress is almost finished, Sager; what if it doesn't fit?"

Mom came to the door calling for us to come in. We raced for the door; I passed my sisters with ease and beat them to Grandma's room; I was ready to prove to them that my story was real and that I had spoken to a little man, all dressed in green with a top hat.

Once we were gathered around the snack drawer in Grandma's room, I could tell by the look on Sager and Elizabeth's faces that they were sure I was about to play a joke on them. They were surprised as I slid open the drawer and pointed to the black pot the little man had left behind.

Elizabeth gasped with excitement. Sager said, "I wonder what else he left behind?" as she pushed past Elizabeth climbing into the drawer first. She inspected the drawer and came out with a green top hat. Clearing her throat, Sager began to bark orders. She said, "Elizabeth, I want this whole room inspected and photographed. Should anything in this room not smell right or you find anything that doesn't belong here, Mr. Wienie and I need to know immediately." Then Sager turned to me and said, "Sit down; tell me again, Wienie, what happened in here this morning. The slightest detail could be a clue."

As I told Sager the events that led me to the little man dressed in green, Elizabeth ran to get her camera. Sager stopped me, saying, "No, Mr. Wienie, you can skip the part about being hungry, and I really don't think your dream of dreams about bacon is a clue." However, when I came to the part about how the little man sang a song to me, Sager interrupted, asking me to sing the song to her.

Tilting her head side to side, Sager stared at me as I mimicked the little man's voice and sang the song he had sung.

"So soon may I follow, when friendships decay, and from love shining circle. The gems drop away. When true hearts lie withered, and fond ones are flown, oh, who would inhabit this bleak world alone."

There was more to the song, but I could only remember the last part. Elizabeth came to sit next to Sager just as I finished the song. She announced that she had photographed the entire room, then pointed to the window, telling us, "I've found a strange scent

Buckles O'Leary

over there." We all agreed that the strange scent around the window smelled the same as the top hat.

We took turns all night watching for the little man dressed in green to return, but he didn't show up. My sisters had a great time taking selfies and being silly. I wondered why girls like to talk about clothes and boys so much. It's always Snoopy this or the Jersey Beach Boys that. Oh, and let's not forget about Prince Elvis!

Apparently, this prince is not an actual prince. Elizabeth informed Sager and me that he is an "Italian Mob Prince," but he's not really an actual prince. I sure hope they don't use all the film before we find this little man dressed in green.

The following day, we were all on high alert, watching for anything that moved. As nightfall approached, I was excited about dinner; hopefully, the little man dressed in green would soon show up. Elizabeth and I lined up when mom called us for dinner, but Sager didn't. She was starving and followed mom into the storage room to help get our food.

Suddenly, Sager let out a howl. She barked for Elizabeth and me to come immediately. Sager said, "Hurry, Elizabeth, grab the camera." I rushed into the storage room just in time to see a little man peering out from behind our food bin.

"I can't get around mom; I'm stuck; she's in the way, Elizabeth barked, then asked, "Where's Wienie?"

Sager screamed, "Brother get in here; come help us!" I tried running between mom's legs but only spun out; thinking fast, I decided to jump between her legs, and that's when mom and I collided.

Our food flew through the air and scattered on the floor. Elizabeth and Sager were both screaming and pointing in different directions, claiming they saw him. I heard Sager ask me if I was okay, then I heard her say, he's over here. Then I heard Elizabeth say no, Sager, he's over here. I got to my feet and scanned the room. Little men dressed in black were standing everywhere. It was evident by how they appeared, then disappeared just as quickly, that they were taunting us.

Chapter 2

AFTER SEEING THE LITTLE MEN DRESSED IN BLACK, Sager and Elizabeth were really quiet as we ate dinner. No boy talk and not even one mention of Sager's new dress. I was worried because the little men dressed in black we had just seen looked nothing like the angelic-faced little man dressed in green, that sang a song to me from Grandma's snack drawer. We had only a few more hours to prepare for tonight. Mom would be heading to bed soon.

As she handed each of us a walkie-talkie, Sager said, "We need to set up watch stations throughout the house." She lowered her voice and began to whisper, "Listen up to you two. If you see that little man dressed in green, the code word will be…."

That's when I screamed the first word that came to my mind, "Bacon!" Sager rolled her eyes at me and said, "Why don't you just scream it a little louder, Wienie? I don't think the neighbors, let alone the little man, quite heard you, but yes, the code word can be bacon.

I'm going to go hide this top hat and pot, then I will take the first watch, and then Mr. Wienie, you're next, and then Elizabeth, you can finish up until morning."

As Sager walked in front of us, she turned on our walkie-talkies. "When speaking on the radio, you need to say your name, state your business, and when you are finished speaking, you need to say, Over." Sager then told us what our call names would be when we used the radio. "Wienie, you are Sausage Dog Lover Lips. I will be Pearl Dog Queen of the Jersey Beach Boys." She finished by saying, "And you, my dear sweet baby sister, are going to be, Red Dog Princess in Waiting."

Usually, this is my favorite time of every day, when mom prepares the house for bedtime. It includes snacks from mom, and I always manage to convince Grandma to give me snacks again; then it's bedtime kisses, and everyone goes to bed. But not tonight; tonight, there would be no snacks; it was go time; I needed to be alert. Elizabeth and I wished Sager good luck; Elizabeth went to bed because she had the last watch, and I headed straight to Grandma's room to wait.

I should have been sleeping, but instead, I lay there staring out the window. I wondered how many more little men were in the house and how long they had been here, not to mention how they even managed to get into our home. I hadn't even realized I had drifted off to sleep; suddenly, I felt something tickle my nose. I opened my eyes, and there stood the little man dressed in green, holding his finger to his mouth, indicating I needed to be quiet and to listen.

He said, "Hello, my friend, my name is Buckles O'Leary. I have come to find a place to hide my pot of gold. `Tis my misfortune that

I have lost my top hat and black pot. I have come to offer you a great many items in exchange for my things."

I shook my head and reached for the walkie-talkie. I started screaming into the radio. But at that moment, I couldn't remember the code word. My heart was pounding, and my mouth went dry. All I could get out was fresh fish, ham, a river of gravy, Grandma's snap-n-pop. Oh, for the love of bacon was running through my head. What was the code word? For the life of me, I couldn't remember the code word.

Sager's voice came over the radio, saying, "This is Pearl Dog Queen of the Jersey Beach Boys. Who is speaking? Over."

I keyed the mic and screamed, "This is Sausage Lips Lover Dog... OVER!!!"

Sager's voice came back over the radio again and said, "We don't know anyone by that name; please try again... Over."

Elizabeth laughed into her radio as she said, "This is Red Dog Princess in Waiting calling Pearl Dog Queen of the Jersey Beach Boys; I believe that was Sausage Dog Lover Lips, Over."

The little man became frustrated and started to leave; I sprang to my feet and snatched him up. I held him down and screamed into the radio, "Oh, for the sake of Pete, I'm in Grandma's room. I have the little man dressed in green."

Sager's voice came over the radio, telling Elizabeth to hurry to Grandma's room. Then her voice trailed off into the distance. The little man struggled to free himself, but I was able to hold him down. He was begging and reminding me he would grant me a great many items if only I would set him free. I could hear Elizabeth running down the hallway. She announced herself as she entered the room, snapping pictures, "It's me, Red Dog Princess in Waiting; where is the little man?"

The flash from the camera was bright, and I closed my eyes; the little man slipped through my paws. "Elizabeth, quick, grab him; he is under your feet!" I screamed.

I repeatedly blinked, trying to focus my eyes again. Elizabeth was still taking photos; the camera's flash made the room look like a scary movie scene. She chased the little man throughout the room and into the hallway. Excited that the chase was on, I ran as fast as possible, following Elizabeth. I just knew she would catch him. Of the three of us, my baby sister is the fastest; she was barking and calling for Sager over the radio. "This is Red Dog Princess in waiting. Where are you, Pearl Dog Queen of the Jersey Beach Boys? We are headed up the hallway to the living room in pursuit of the little man. Over."

I was on Elizabeth's heels; we were fast closing in on the little man. As we rounded the corner into the living room, I caught the scent of bacon and stopped. I sniffed the floor, and to my surprise, a trail of bacon was leading toward mom's room. I was in complete shock. The dream of all my dreams now lay before me.

As I took that first step toward the trail of bacon, the last thing I remember hearing was Elizabeth calling my name over the radio. She screamed, "Sausage Dog Lover Lips, I'm in the kitchen; I need reinforcements! Pearl Dog Queen of the Jersey Beach Boys, I have the little man at bay on the table! Where are you?" I could hear Elizabeth's voice come over the radio again, "Hello! It's me, Red Dog Princess in Waiting. I have the little man! Bacon! Over!"

The trail of bacon was calling me, beckoning me onward with each step; the tender bites of bacon became more than I could resist. I responded over the radio back to Elizabeth, "Yes! Bacon! Bacon! Bacon!" As I licked my lips, I said, "Over!"

I knew I should continue helping my sister, but then there was another piece of juicy bacon, and then another; the trail went as far as the eye could see. I was in heaven when suddenly I heard a door close behind me. I was trapped. That glorious path of bacon had led me to mom's closet.

Chapter 3

ELIZABETH WAS REALLY WORKED UP NOW, SCREAMING for Sager over the radio, wanting to know where I had gone. She said, "Why is this little man, who calls himself Buckles O'Leary, dancing and singing in front of me?"

I started to answer Elizabeth when another piece of bacon appeared in front of me from under the door. It was wonderful. Who would have thought that mom's closet held so many treasures? Why can't I have a door like this that dispenses bacon in Grandma's room? All I had to do was reach for my radio, and another piece of bacon would appear from under the door. I lay there relaxing on my side, eating bite after bite, listening to Elizabeth as she described what was happening.

Elizabeth returned on the radio and said, "This is Red Dog Princess, and I'm tired of Waiting; Buckles O'Leary wants to know where we put his black pot and top hat. What should I tell him… OVER?"

At that moment, the bacon pieces appeared two and three at a time. I couldn't keep up with this wonderful bacon feeding door. My mouth was full as I responded, "This is Sausage Dog Lover Lips, Pearl Dog Queen of the Jersey Beach Boys has hidden the items." Another piece of bacon appeared as I said, "Over!"

Elizabeth sounded irritated as she barked, "This is Red Dog; never mind! Where are you, Wienie, and what are you eating… Over!?"

Suddenly a stranger's voice came over the radio; I could hear Sager in the background; she sounded muffled and mad. The stranger said, "I am Clurichaun! We have Your Queen of the Jersey Beach Boys."

Buckles O'Leary's voice sounded light-hearted; this voice was different. His tone was in no way light-hearted, and he had not sung his words. I thought to myself, who else was in the house. White noise was the only sound now; Elizabeth had stopped calling on the radio.

Pacing back and forth, I began to worry. I was so frustrated that I had let myself be tricked by bacon and got captured in mom's closet. I dug at the carpet, trying to free myself. It was useless; I was trapped. Every few seconds, another piece of bacon would appear. I pretended to eat the bacon by smacking my lips and then hiding it behind me in the closet. I suddenly remembered the song Buckles O'Leary had sung and why he was here. The song was something along the lines of they only come to hide their treasure. But why would they want to take Sager? They must have watched, heard our plans, and known our code names. After all, Sager knows the rules of war; you never give your true name.

I threw myself on my side and wished we were only playing pretend while in the yard, but this was real. Now, someone has Sager; did they hurt her? Did they trap her like they did me? She sounded muffled. Did they have her tied up, or even worse, in a cage? I remembered how Sager had told me she sat locked in a cage for four months before she was rescued and came to live with our mom.

Feeling bad for allowing my obsession with bacon to overcome me, I leaped to my feet; they were not going to put my sister in a cage! I charged the door, ready to claw and scratch my way out. I dug at the door and the carpet like a wild animal, determined to get out, but it was no use. Feeling defeated, I sat down. I reached for the radio and tried to speak, but all I could get out was one long howl. I sat there listening closely, hoping to hear Elizabeth or even the stranger's voice again. Still, the only sound that could be heard was the haunting silence. Feeling hopeless and lost, wishing someone would hear me and open the door, I continued to howl.

Suddenly, I saw the door handle move. I could hear a commotion on the other side of the door. The door handle moved again. I jumped up, growling and kicking my hind feet, preparing for war. They took me once, but I wasn't going easy this time; I didn't care what food they placed in front of me. The door handle shook and shook, then the door slowly swung open. Elizabeth stepped from the shadows and said, "Wienie, Sager is right about you; all you really think about is food." I whined, running to her, relieved to know she was safe. Then I saw Buckles O'Leary standing on her back. I lunged forward, snatching him off her back, furiously shaking him. "No, Wienie, don't. Buckles is helping us." Elizabeth said as she continued to explain. "He is not the one that has Sager; it's his evil cousins; they took her." Then she grabbed Buckle's legs and tried to pull him from my grasp. I stopped shaking him. He looked at me and gave me a half-smile as I placed him on the floor. Adjusting his clothes, he explained why he had come here. He said, "When you first saw me, I was here to hide my pot of gold in your Grandma's room. I was unaware that my cousins had followed me; I know this because they are afraid to go in there."

I could understand why Buckles would want to hide his treasures in my Grandma's room. I loved it in there; it was always warm and cozy, with plenty of snacks to eat.

Buckles peeked out the door, then turned back toward us; he said, "My cousins have a terrible temper; they like to play tricks on those they choose to prey on. They can only take what they see by having it given to them. I spend all day making shoes for the fairies, and at night I hide my gold; it's protected by magic from the Kissing Tree in my realm. This is why no one can ever find it. The night you found me in your Grandma's snack drawer, I was hiding my gold. My cousins must have seen the pearls on your sister Sager's neck, and now they want them at any cost. Precious gems and stones are what they need to travel the realms. They spend most of their days at home in pubs drinking Irish Whiskey."

Elizabeth interrupted and stated, "We need to get out of here and hide before they come back and trap us too."

My head was spinning, and my stomach was starting to ache; maybe it was from all the bacon. I had questions for Buckles O'Leary, but we could hear footsteps approaching. Quickly, we left the closet and hid under mom's bed. We watched as a little man dressed in black placed more bacon under the closet door. Suspicious that it had not disappeared, the evil leprechaun listened as he peered under the door. My stomach began to ache again; I whined; Elizabeth looked at me, fully aware of what would happen. She patted my belly and shaking her head no, she whispered, "No, Wienie, not now; he will hear you and find us."

Another cramp came, and a bead of sweat dripped from my forehead when it happened. The bacon had caught up with me; I had the wiener wind, as Grandma calls it; it was loud and smelled terrible. The evil leprechaun jerked his head in our direction and searched the room with his eyes. His face was wrinkled, with a big ugly nose and his eyes were bloodshot. We could hear him breathing as he came closer to the bed. Elizabeth held her paw to her mouth, and Buckles lay pinching his nose. The smell was more than we would take, and we were thankful when the evil leprechaun finally left the room.

We came out from under the bed; my sister was fanning her nose, asking me, "How much bacon have you eaten tonight, Wienie?"

I chuckled and said, "Now that you've asked, obviously, just enough." I felt better and was ready to get back to finding Sager. I asked Buckles why his cousins feared our Grandma's room. He said, "The rainbow holds all kinds of extraordinary charms." He did a little dance and spun in a circle on his heel. Lowering his voice to a whisper, he said, "Anyone or anything can cross the rainbow bridge to this realm, but it's only the true of heart that can return to our realm unpaid. This is why they want your sister's pearls. They need them to return to our land. They fear your Grandma's room because it is a happy place where joy and laughter can be seen, heard, and felt." I felt enchanted watching Buckles speak with such glee about our Grandma's room.

Buckles continued his explanation, "I needed to see what brings you such pleasure and joy every day, Mr. Wienie. So, I opened the snack drawer to peek in; that's when you woke and found me. 'Tis my top hat and black pot that make the rainbow appear and give good leprechauns magic. I was able to hide unseen by you until you crawled into the drawer. Now that I have had the misfortune of losing my items, the rainbow is open, and I have no magic. This is how my cousins have come to be here, free to play their tricks on whomever they please. They gather treasures to spend in the pubs back home. Only the blackest of hearts must pay their way in both directions to and from any of the realms. Unless they manage to steal a ride unseen by the Gatekeeper, they must pay with precious gems and stones. 'Tis my top hat that allows me to travel the realms; alas, I, too, am trapped in this land."

Elizabeth and I sat listening to Buckles' story; I had heard of a place called 'somewhere over the rainbow' but never believed it was a real place. I took in every detail, as we needed all the information we could get. Not only did we need to get Sager back with her pearls, but we had to find Buckles' top hat and black pot so he, too, could return to his land. We devised a plan and headed for Grandma's room. Hopefully, soon we will have Sager back. We watched as Buckles disappeared into the living room; he said he would give us a thumbs up if all was clear.

Buckles waved, giving us the thumbs up. "There's the signal, Elizabeth; let's go." I said aloud. Keeping my sister behind me, we snuck slowly out into the living room. It was dark as I nosed my way along the wall; we were making good time. We had made it to the hallway, and I could see one of the evil cousins was standing guard at the entrance of Grandma's room. I turned and whispered to Elizabeth, "We have to turn back and go through the kitchen."

"How are we going to get them away from the door?" She asked. "Why do I always have to know everything Elizabeth," I snapped back.

Buckles had caught up to us, telling us he found where they were holding Sager. She was locked in a cage in our storage room. He said, "They haven't been able to get your sister to give them her pearl neckless. My cousins are taking turns reading love letters to someone named Snoopy. I believe they are torturing her with a diary."

Elizabeth's hair raised on her neck; she was becoming enraged now. Bearing her teeth, she said, "How dare they read the babysitter's diary, they have just gone way too far." At this moment, Elizabeth tried to run past me; she was willing to face down these evil leprechauns and rescue Sager all by herself. I grabbed her tail to hold her back. I said, "We have already read Sager's diary. It's no big deal, Elizabeth."

Hanging her head Elizabeth looked ashamed; she sat down as she whispered, "Wienie, Sager started another diary, and I've already peeked at it."

I looked into Elizabeth's eyes, unsure of what I heard. She took a deep breath and said, "The first night we were on watch for Buckles, I read it because I knew Sager was on watch and wouldn't catch me. The evil leprechauns must have seen the dairy too."

Buckles interrupted, asking, "Would Sager have hidden my top hat and black pot with her diary?" Ignoring Buckles, I stared at Elizabeth; feeling a little overwhelmed and left out, I said, "You mean to tell me that Sager started a new diary, and you didn't tell me. We promised never to snoop in her bed again. Now here you are with another secret that I know nothing about!"

Elizabeth sprang to her feet and barked, "You left the mission because you are obsessed with food. You don't get to yell at me!"

I held up my paw and said, "We are gonna circle back to this; we need to discuss half your snacks for the rest of the month."

"For three months, I tolerated you taking half my snacks when we found the first diary Sager wrote, not to mention your unhealthy obsession with bacon. You and your wiener wind that Grandma thinks is so cute!" Elizabeth said through bared teeth.

My baby sister and I had never yelled at each other before; I was beginning to feel very angry and blurted out, "You nosey Ginger!"

Elizabeth got in my face and yelled, "Let me tell you, Wienie, you stink, and I bet you would eat cat poop if someone rolled it in bacon!"

Buckles wiggled his way between my sister and me and said, "You two need to quiet down; if you don't stop, you will conjure a Banshee to this land. Remember, the rainbow is open and unprotected."

I stopped and looked at Buckles; as Elizabeth said, "What?" Buckles pulled both of us closer to him and whispered, "You are only fighting because of the evil that follows my cousins. Making everyone fight is how they get you to give them what they want." Elizabeth apologized to me, and I mouthed the words, 'we will circle back to this one.'

Buckles turned and headed toward the kitchen table. As he led the way, he explained the dangers of Banshees; he said, "They are shadows of no shadows. They are the faces of many faces that have no faces. When loved ones continue to argue and lose faith in each other, a Banshee will appear.

He was singing his words again and talking in riddles; Elizabeth looked back at me and shrugged her shoulders as she whispered, "Let me guess, only love kills the demon." Then she rolled her eyes, and when she turned back toward Buckles, she bumped into him. He had his hands on his hips and said to her, "Yes, you silly Ginger, love is all it takes to kill the demon! Now come here." Buckles kissed her on the nose, and she shook her head, saying, "Oh Wienie, I am sorry, brother, come here."

Elizabeth came to hug me and kiss my nose; I pushed her away and reminded her that she said I stunk like wiener wind. As she kissed my nose anyway, I felt the anger wash away. I stood there looking into her eyes; how could we have been so hateful to each other? We needed to get Sager back and make these evil leprechauns disappear.

I felt better as we headed to the kitchen; I was thankful that Elizabeth's radio was still on the table. The evil cousin had my radio and was fully aware that I had escaped from mom's closet. We listened as they talked back and forth, using mine and Sager's walkie-talkies. I am sure they heard Elizabeth and me fighting; they were laughing and repeating the hateful words we had said to each other. Their laughter sent cold shivers down my spine after I heard one of them say that they thought Sager would give up and hand over the pearls because she had stopped growling and was speaking to them.

Buckles explained that if his cousins were to find his top hat and black pot, they could control the rainbow, and it would be for the worst in every realm. He told us no longer would the luck of the Irish exist, and all happiness would be consumed by selfishness. He said, "If I only had my hat, then I would have my magical powers back. I could trick them, sending them back through the rainbow unpaid."

Elizabeth began to cry; she could see I was afraid because Buckles had talked fast again, and neither of us understood him, "Unpaid, what does that mean?" I asked.

Buckles explained, "When you ride the rainbow to any of the realms, all must be paid one way or another. The evil ones have no light. This is why they must pay the Gatekeeper with treasures. Once in a lifetime, a good leprechaun can pay the price for another. The price we pay is why the rainbow colors are so bright, spun in the songs of love and sacrifice."

Footsteps could be heard everywhere in the house now. The evil leprechauns searched high and low. They must have left Sager unattended because we heard her on the radio clearly say, "Attention Savages, you will find a black pot never ever under a hairy thing, but that which rides on my head and hides my dreams shall be found within and under all things." Sager's voice faded in the distance; she sounded muffled again as she growled. Elizabeth held her paws to her mouth and said, "Wienie, Sager is turning into one of them. She is talking in circles."

Doing my best to comfort Elizabeth, I sat there thinking about what I had just heard Sager say. Then it hit me; I repeated aloud, "A hairy thing and found within and under all things!" As if I had cured the world of all wrongdoings, I said, "No, Elizabeth, Sager is brilliant. She just told us where to find the top hat."

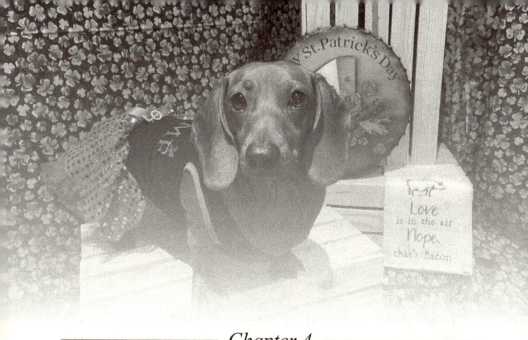

Chapter 4

I FELT HOPEFUL AGAIN; SAGER HAD MANAGED TO TELL US over the radio where we could find Buckles' top hat and black pot. I asked Buckles to take Elizabeth with him to check on Sager and to try to let her know we had heard her message. I told him that I would meet them back at the table when they were finished with that.

I carefully made my way to the living room. At that moment, I took a deep breath and hoped I was correct about Sager's riddle and finding the top hat under the couch. I was pretty sure Sager was talking about mom's brown furry blanket. We all love that blanket; Sager, Elizabeth, and I have had many good naps on it.

I heard footsteps again; I jumped onto the sofa and hid under the furry blanket. I listened to two of the evil cousins as they searched the living room, looking for me. One of them said, "I wonder why this Queen of the Jersey Beach Boys doesn't like bacon like that fat one does?" I held my breath.

The fat one, I thought. Elizabeth is not overweight, and I don't think she ate any bacon tonight. The other one laughed and said, "Soon, we will have the hat and be free to ride the rainbow as we choose." I could hear them moving things around in the room, then they stepped onto the blanket. Both were now standing on my back. I smelled the stench of Irish Whiskey as they bragged about how famous they would be at the pubs once they had Buckles' treasures and his top hat.

I was nervous, and my stomach began to growl, and they heard it. It was going to happen again, wiener wind; I squeezed my eyes shut, afraid of how loud it would sound, and then they would find me. I thanked the bacon gods because it was silent but deadly. It lingered in the blanket at first, and I resisted coughing. The two evil leprechauns began accusing each other of the stench. Still arguing, they headed for mom's room.

Feeling relieved that they were gone, my stomach stopped cramping. I wiggled off the sofa and onto the floor. Searching under the sofa for the top hat, I found it sparkling in the dark, just like Sager said it would be. I reached for it, but it was just out of my grasp. Laying on my side, I clawed at the carpet, trying to grasp the hat. Sucking in my breath and kicking with my hind legs, I slid further under the couch. Just a few more inches and I would have the hat. Finally, I had the hat; I tried to back up, but I was stuck. The evil leprechauns returned to the room. I heard them say, look, it's the fat one.

I pulled and pulled, trying to free myself; my stomach was cramping, and they were closing in. I sucked in with all my might as I sprang out from under the couch. Not only was I free, but my cramps went away. I stood face to face with them; as they fanned the air in front of their noses. The two evil leprechauns began circling me and offered me bacon again. I backed up and leaped into the air. The hat began to glow and shake. I realized I was flying; it was marvelous. Buckles was right; his hat, indeed, was magical. I felt weightless as I hovered above them. My stomach cramped again, and I dropped the hat; I was falling. I watched as the evil leprechauns picked up the hat. They laughed and started to leave.

As I scrambled to my feet, Elizabeth appeared out of the darkness with Buckles on her back. She snatched the hat away from the evil leprechauns. She ran down the hallway, through the kitchen, and back around again. The top hat sparkled in the darkness as gold glitter spread throughout the air. The chase was on, but they couldn't catch her. Every time they were close to grabbing her, she would leap into the air and fly for a short distance. On her second lap through the house, they trapped her by throwing mom's furry blanket on top of her. I ran to help, and that's when Buckles put on his hat. He did a little dance as the gold glitter shimmered down his body. He was glowing. Elizabeth was covered in gold dust from the hat. He held up his hand and said, "Oh, what a merry chase this be; where and who would I be if you came and caught me?"

Buckles' evil cousins stopped and scratched their heads as they tried to figure out his riddle. Then Elizabeth and Buckles disappeared into thin air. I dashed behind the couch when Elizabeth and Buckles disappeared. The evil leprechauns returned to the storage room, and I ran to get a peek while the door was still open. I could see they had Sager gagged, and all four of her feet were tied together. What did the riddle Buckles had recited before he disappeared with my sister mean? I felt afraid, and I wanted to go and hide in Grandma's bed.

I wished this was only a bad dream and I would wake up to mom's call that breakfast was being served.

I returned to the kitchen table, hoping Elizabeth would be there with Buckles. I whispered into the darkness, "Elizabeth, Buckles, where are you? I am here; come out." They were nowhere to be seen. I waited for what seemed to be hours, then I remembered Elizabeth's radio was still lying on the table. I thought about confronting the evil leprechauns when an angry voice came over the radio. I jumped up to listen. They said, "If this Queen of the Jersey Beach Boys is not going to give up her pearls, we will take her with us. We are moving her to the gate in the Grandma's room."

I stood there thinking oh no, they were going to take Sager through the rainbow. What did Buckles mean when he said, where and who would I be if you came and caught me?

The storage room door opened; seven evil leprechauns emerged from the room. They were carrying my sister, gagged and strapped upside down to a pole. She was growling and struggling. I felt helpless as I watched them threaten to poke her with their tiny swords. One of them said, "No need to worry, Queen of the Jersey Beach Boys; once we ride the rainbow, you will never again see this realm or any who reside in it." He looked to the heavens and laughed, then said, "Yes indeed, you are the treasure we need; with you being a Queen, we will arrive unseen."

Suddenly, Elizabeth and Buckles appeared out of nowhere in front of me. Elizabeth was still sparkling from the glitter from Buckles' hat. She smelled of 1001 adventures and had a tiny four-leaf clover tied around her neck. She was excited and tried to explain where they had gone as she hugged me. "Wienie, look what I have." Elizabeth said, pointing to the clover. I held up my paw, interrupting her, and told Buckles, "Sager won't give up her pearls, so now your cousins are taking her with them."

Buckles listened closely as I recalled everything I heard his evil cousin say as they made their way to Grandma's room. Buckles sounded worried and said, "If they take your sister with them, she can never come back; soon, she will forget the love of this world and become one of them. We must get to the gate before they do." Buckles took my paw and then Elizabeth's in each of his hands, and the next thing I knew, we were standing in Grandma's room next to the window.

Buckles was glowing from head to toe now; he said, "'Tis the start of the rainbow, my friends, do not stray too close, for the gate will open soon." He took off his hat and bowed to the wall as he said, "Gatekeeper, Gatekeeper, listen to me; 'tis Buckles O'Leary; open for me." The room began to shake, the wall opened up, and a rainbow filled Grandma's room.

Buckles stood and placed his hat back on his head; he reminded us not to stray into the light. My sister and I were in awe at all the beautiful colors. That's when Elizabeth screamed. Quickly I turned around as two of the evil leprechauns held their tiny swords to Elizabeth's throat. The cousins had made their way into Grandma's room. They were determined to leave with Sager.

All the evil cousins laughed as the one in charge pointed to the four-leaf clover hanging around Elizabeth's neck and said, "With this one, tonight and all nights, we ride free as the Gatekeeper sees."

Sager managed to wiggle out of her gag. Growling and baring her teeth, she yelled for them to let Elizabeth go. Sager told them she would give up her pearls if they would release our baby sister. They no longer needed the pearls because they could ride free with the four-leaf clover. The evil leprechaun pointed to the four-leaf clover and said, "Do you see what I see, 'tis the Gatekeepers key."

I felt powerless as they held their tiny swords to Elizabeth's neck. They were forcing her toward the rainbow. She was inches from riding the colors. I threw my head back, letting out a loud howl. Sager was screaming for me to save our baby sister; she was crying and begging the evil leprechauns to take her instead.

Buckles yelled as he stood in front of the gate to the rainbow protecting it. "Gatekeeper, Gatekeeper, O'hear me somehow, let them sing songs of what I must do now." Buckles took his top hat off and threw it into the rainbow. The room shook again as different colored lights emerged from the gate. The lights were dark, and they screamed as they searched the room. Then the lights grabbed each of the seven evil leprechauns, dragging them grudgingly back into the rainbow. I lunged forward, grabbed Elizabeth by the collar, and snatched her from them. I threw her toward Sager and shielded my sisters from the lights. The gate exploded with a final ear-splitting scream, and the wall closed. The room became silent; gold dust and glitter now filled the air.

Elizabeth had freed Sager; as I looked for Buckles, he was nowhere to be seen. I wondered if he had also been pulled into the river of color, sending him back over the rainbow. That's when we saw Buckles leaning against the wall; we ran to him. Kneeling beside Buckles, Elizabeth asked if he was okay; Buckles didn't move. Frantic, Elizabeth shook him as she begged him to open his eyes.

The sparkle that once glimmered over his body was now slipping away. Turning to me, Elizabeth pleaded with her eyes for me to do something. "I don't understand." Elizabeth said as she looked from me to Sager.

Sager touched our baby sister's paw and said, "He's gone, sister." Elizabeth backed away, covering her mouth while shaking her head; she sobbed, "No, no, he can't be gone."

Buckles had sacrificed his life for us; he paid the Gatekeeper with his own life. Elizabeth and Sager wept as I sang the song Buckles first sang to me.

"So soon may I follow, When friendships decay, And from Love's shining circle. The gems drop away. When true hearts lie, withered And fond ones are flown, Oh, who would inhabit this bleak world alone."

I wasn't sure what the song meant or even if it was a happy one. Buckles had told me it was a song from long ago. It was the only thing I could think to do at the moment. Elizabeth pulled away from Sager and lay beside Buckles with her paw in his hand. She wept as she said Buckles was her friend; tears rolled down her cheeks; she lifted her head and began to howl. My baby sister's pain was more than I could take; I lifted my head and let out a long howl, Sager joined me, and we all howled again for our little friend that had given his life for ours.

Suddenly, I noticed that Buckles appeared to be glowing. I stopped howling and watched as Elizabeth and Sager continued to howl. They sang our song, the sad song from long ago when wolves walked alone. Each howl became longer and deeper from their love for our friend. Sager harmonized with Elizabeth's sorrow.

Then Buckles sparkled; could it be that they were bringing him back from a world unknown? Sager and Elizabeth's eyes were closed as they continued this haunting howl of sorrow. I howled again in tune with them. Buckles was glowing now. I stepped forward and said aloud, "That's it! For the love of bacon-filled closets."

Then I howled with all my might right in Buckles' face. He coughed and opened his eyes. Elizabeth quickly sat up and began to lick his face. Sager threw her head back to howl again and opened her eyes. Our tears of sorrow were now overcome with sounds of joy and happiness. Elizabeth squealed delightedly and said, "How, why, what happened?"

Buckles explained that he had to sacrifice his life to send his evil cousins back through the rainbow unpaid. This way, they could never return to our world. He said our love brought him back from the shadows of the unknown.

This was when we learned that when Elizabeth and Buckles disappeared, they had returned to the land of the Kissing Tree. Elizabeth had healed the Kissing Tree with her love. The leprechauns enchanted the four-leaf clover with magic as a reward, but that's a story for another time. We asked Buckles how he would return home. I said, "The Gate to the Rainbow was destroyed when it took your cousins." Pointing to the four-leaf clover still hanging from our sister's neck, Buckles O'Leary spun on his heel and said, "With my black pot and the Gatekeeper's key, 'tis the Luck 'O the Irish, is all we need." He laid his hand on Elizabeth's back, they smiled impishly at each other, then winked at Sager and me, and they both disappeared.

The End
Or is it?

Dance of The Sugar Plum Wienie

Written By:

Cendy J. Hatfield

Chapter 1

"**H**E SPRANG TO HIS SLEIGH, TO HIS TEAM HE GAVE A whistle,
And away they all flew like the down of a thistle.
But I heard him exclaim, as he drove out of sight—Happy Christmas to all, and to all a good night!" Sager said, then added, "Now go to sleep, both of you! Santa won't bring our presents tomorrow night if we don't go to bed on time; you know he sees us when we are sleeping."

Sager closed her favorite Christmas story, 'The Night Before Christmas,' by Clement C. Moore, then kissed me on the forehead. She snuggled my cheek and said, "Merry Christmas, Elizabeth James. I love you, baby sister."

I closed my eyes immediately and giggled while I pretended to be fast asleep. Sager smiled while she kissed Wienie on his forehead and shook her paw at both of us as she left our dad's office. She headed upstairs to get in her big bed at the foot of our mom and dad's bed.

I could tell Mr. Wienie was already asleep; he was making grunting sounds and funny little biting movements with his teeth. He was muttering something about Jessica. Jessica is a bacon-wrapped dumpling. Our silly brother always says if Jessica was real instead of food, she would be the perfect soul-mate for him.

I could hear Sager's toenails click on the hardwood floor as she crossed the living room. I wiggled out of bed and crawled to the office doorway. I watched my sister stop to sniff one of her presents under the Christmas tree. It was a big box from Mr. Wienie and me wrapped in old-fashioned Santa Claus paper with a red velvet bow. I sure hoped she liked what we picked out for her. Sager scratched at her collar, then continued around the big oak newel post and up the stairs to the second floor to our parents' suite of rooms.

I lay with my head on my paws, watching the lights chasing up and down the Christmas tree, and I loved seeing the reflection of the fireplace looking so shiny on the hardwood floor. The softly glowing lights and Christmas decorations made our home feel warm and cozy. On each side of the fireplace was a tall wooden soldier, just like mom had at home, and our stockings were hanging on the mantel. Mom had set up a small table so we could put Christmas cookies and carrots out for Santa and his reindeer.

I'm not sure how long I lay watching the lights on the Christmas tree when suddenly, out of the corner of my eye, I saw something move. It looked like wings and tiny moss-covered shoes. I sat very still, holding my breath, then I saw it again. It moved as though it had been flying in and out of the tree for days. It floated around the room close to the floor, then disappeared back into the Christmas tree.

I sat up and rubbed the sleep from my eyes; they were so droopy I almost missed it. I looked again and thought maybe I was dreaming.

But whatever it was, it moved one of mom's crystal heart ornaments as it disappeared among the tree branches. I held my breath, darting my eyes, looking all around the Christmas tree, but the only thing I could see was the crystal heart swinging back and forth.

I awoke the following morning, still lying in the doorway of dad's office. I had sat for what felt like hours staring at the Christmas tree and hadn't realized I had fallen asleep. When I opened my eyes, I could see through the big windows that went from ceiling to floor; it was snowing outside. Large white snowflakes gently floated down and piled higher on the already deep snow in the yard.

Not realizing my brother was still in his bed, I said aloud, "That's strange; I didn't know it could snow while the sun was shining."

From his bed, in the corner of dad's office, Mr. Wienie said, "The sun has been up for hours, Elizabeth; why were you sleeping in the doorway?"

Sager, Mr. Wienie, and I love to play in our dad's office while he is conducting business; this room is the warmest because of the fireplace. As a matter of fact, there's a fireplace in almost every room of our home here in Alaska. There's even a fireplace outside where the hot tub is. Sager calls it a big boiling bathtub because she hates taking a bath. My dad says that this fireplace eats wood like Mr. Wienie eats bacon. Popping and snapping while it eats up the pitch-covered wood.

My dad is so funny when he talks on his phone; he likes to cuss a lot. Sometimes he calls mom on the phone and asks her to make him a cheese sandwich; he says, "Hold the crusts, put extra cheese on it, and bring something for my three little outlaws to eat. They are powerfully hungry and need plenty of nourishment to be the true savages they are meant to be." When my dad says this, it always makes Mr. Wienie's tail wag, and he licks his lips. The funny thing about this is our mom is in the kitchen just a few rooms away.

Snow was falling to the ground, like a million tiny diamonds floating everywhere in the morning sunshine. I got up from my warm spot in the doorway, stretched, and jumped to the window seat. I licked the window to see if my tongue would stick like that kid's tongue did in the movie we watched last night, 'A Christmas Story,' but no such luck; my tongue didn't stick. So, I said, "Oh well, I guess I'll try licking something else outside."

I looked down at Mr. Wienie; he had gone back to sleep and was now lying on his back with his head covered. "Get up, brother." I said as I jumped from the window seat and onto his bed.

I jumped up and down, pulling the blanket off of him. All the while yelling, "Get up, brother, it's Christmas Eve! Santa rides tonight, and as dad says, Santa is going to kiss Mrs. Claus once for me and smack Rudolph on his ass, then slide his cookie-eating ass down our chimney tonight."

I just couldn't seem to say 'ass' enough. Then I remembered what I saw last night. I jumped over Mr. Wienie, he was still lying in bed and headed for the Christmas Tree. Mr. Wienie called out, reminding me, "Sager said you need to stop repeating what our dad says! It isn't very ladylike, and dad is the only one who gets to say the word ass."

I felt a slight twinge of guilt when my brother told me it wasn't ladylike to swear. Ever since I watched 'A Christmas Story 2,' I really love to cuss. If those kids in that movie can swear, so can I. Besides that, the dad in the movie cussed up a storm, and my dad cusses, too, only never in front of my grandma.

Suddenly I remembered seeing something flying in and out of the branches of our Christmas tree last night. My heart was pounding as

Dance of The Sugar Plum Wienie

the image of shiny wings, and those tiny moss-covered shoes flashed through my mind.

Feeling my muscles bunch, I flew like the down of a thistle, running toward the Christmas tree. It was like in the story Sager read to us last night; I thought maybe I could fly like Santa's reindeer. "Be the reindeer." I said; I was leaping and pretending to look down as I imagined myself running higher and higher into the air pulling Santa's sleigh. All I needed was jingle bells and a bright red nose. That's when I started to sing, "Elizabeth the red coat Doxie, had a very shiny coat, and if you ever saw her, you would even say...."

I wasn't paying attention to how fast I was running or how close I was to the Christmas tree; I slid right under the tree as I tried to stop. I bumped into a few presents, causing the golden bells to chime loudly as the tree swayed back and forth.

Suddenly the sounds coming from underneath our Christmas tree sounded completely different from the usual sounds inside our home; it was strange. I could hear Christmas music; it was faint, and I could smell cinnamon and hot chocolate. I sniffed again, and sure enough, I could even smell marshmallows. Yummy marshmallows that melt in hot chocolate smothered with cinnamon. The packages under the tree looked like they went on forever. Ribbons and bows and sparkling paper. Big packages and small ones. The sight of it made my eyes grow and my heart thump louder.

I thought to myself, why hadn't I laid under the Christmas tree before? I said, "I'll have to tell Wienie about this spot later. I wonder what he'll think of it." I moved a little further under the Christmas tree to find the spot where I had seen those shimmering wings and tiny moss-covered shoes flying around. "I bet what I saw last night was nothing more than a damn old bug with moss on its feet." I said aloud. Carefully moving a few more Christmas presents out of the way, I asked myself aloud, "Who knew that bugs here in Alaska wore moss-covered shoes?"

"I'm not a bug." I heard someone or something say from far above me, then I heard, "You're a silly Ginger!"

The sound of the voice was like listening to the chiming of many tiny silver bells. Sniffing, I pushed my head further upward to the next set of limbs, saying, "Hello, where are you? What are you? I saw you last night. What are you doing in my Christmas Tree?" I yelled. Standing on my hind feet, I listened as my heart continued to pound, only this time with curiosity.

Wondering where the voice came from, I struggled to see higher up into the tree when Sager's face appeared through the boughs, asking, "Elizabeth, what are you doing in the Christmas Tree? Mom will not be happy if you break her new ornaments. Not to mention you're standing on all the presents."

Before I could tell Sager what I had seen last night and that I just now heard a tiny voice speak to me, Mr. Wienie ran by, announcing breakfast was being served. "Hey, breakfast, bacon, served, about to happen!" Our silly brother was so excited about breakfast that everything he said came out jumbled.

"Come on, Elizabeth, let's get our good morning kisses from dad and mom. I won't tell on you, this time. It's Christmas Eve, plus we get to see Santa this afternoon." Sager said. She gently lifted the garland and lights, helping me to crawl from under the tree without breaking anything.

"Elizabeth James, now you stay out from under our Christmas tree. If you must play around a tree, have Wienie take you outside." Sager scolded over her shoulder as she led the way to the kitchen.

Following Sager to the kitchen, I reminded myself not to forget to tell Mr. Wienie about what I saw and heard in our Christmas tree.

Between bites of breakfast, I told Mr. Wienie about what I had heard this morning and saw last night. He told me it was a dream, or maybe I had too many Christmas cookies. But he stopped eating when I explained that I could hear music and smelled cinnamon and hot chocolate. He raised his head from his breakfast bowl, looked at me, and whispered, "I want to smell hot chocolate too." His eyes were wistful, then he added, "Should we find any bacon or smell any hot chocolate, I get to have the first bites, or I'll tell Sager that you said the ass word twice this morning."

I nodded okay; it didn't matter who got the first bites. What mattered was I had a plan, and my brother was willing to help me find the voice in the Christmas tree.

We could hear dad moving throughout the house, adding wood, and poking at all of the fireplaces; it was the perfect time for me to crawl under our Christmas tree. Mr. Wienie held up the garland and twinkle lights for me to crawl under. I looked back to ensure he was lying down beside the tree to be my lookout. I didn't want Sager to catch me and tell mom. I had already gotten in trouble the day we arrived here for cussing, and I didn't need any more problems.

As I crawled deeper into the tree, I started to hear the sound of Christmas music playing. Only this time, with it, I could hear tiny hammers and what sounded like boxes being wrapped with paper. I sniffed, and much to my surprise, I could smell gingerbread cookies and hot chocolate. It made my mouth water, and I could almost taste the marshmallows. I just loved drinking hot chocolate and eating gingerbread cookies. Pausing for a split second, I thought, shit, what if I can't wait for Mr. Wienie and I accidentally eat a gingerbread cookie without him. Then the smells of all my favorite Christmas goodies took over my thoughts. I've already broken my promise to Sager about cussing; I said the ass word twice today, and so did Mr. Wienie. Convincing myself, thinking if I break down and eat a gingerbread man before my brother and he gets mad, I'll just tell on him for cussing.

The plan I made was working, and everything was going well. I could still see Mr. Wienie's tail where he lay just outside the edge of the Christmas tree. I took a deep breath and sat up to look over the tops of the packages. I started calling out to the voice that had talked to me just before breakfast. "Hello! Please come talk to me. Hello." I called out, listening for a reply, but I only heard music. It sounded like mom's favorite Christmas song. As I hummed the carol, I climbed to the tree branch in front of me, then another branch, and then another. The tiny golden bells hanging from the tree chimed as I climbed higher. The whole tree shook under my weight. Before I lost my nerve, I called out again; only this time, I asked to speak to the little bug that had called me a silly ginger.

The pinecones and flocking on the tree started to fall all over my face and body. I had to stop climbing; I was afraid the tree would fall and then I would really be in trouble. As I looked down, I pleaded, "Please, little bug, come out and talk to me; I'm going to be in so much trouble." Then I held my breath and listened. It was no use; maybe Mr. Wienie was right; I must have imagined it all.

Then I shouted loudly to Mr. Wienie, "Is anyone around? I'm coming back down; I need to get out of this tree." I waited and listened. He didn't answer me. "Brother, answer me!" I yelled again. I thought that maybe he couldn't hear me over the music coming from inside the tree. I pushed my head through the tree branches to see what he was doing. I could see that my brother was lying on the floor, and his eyes were closed. "Damn it! That ass has fallen asleep again." I said loudly.

That's when I saw three tiny plum-shaped bugs approaching Mr. Wienie. My eyes bulged as I watched the three of them lift my brother's lip; they rubbed at his white teeth, laughing and pointing to the sharp points of his canine teeth. Mr. Wienie likes to call those his vampire teeth. "Hey, you bugs!" I shouted loudly. How dare they poke and prod around on my big brother while I was still trying to get out of the Christmas Tree. At this point, I was sure I was making a huge mess. Knowing if I got caught by Sager, I wouldn't get any snacks later. "Hey, stop being a horse's ass, and answer me!" I shouted. Suddenly feeling very angry, I couldn't control myself; I growled and started barking.

Finally, the tallest of the three fat bugs looked up at me. The bug smiled and then rubbed her hands together. I could tell she was a girl, but; then I realized they were not bugs at all; instead, they looked like sugar plums with wings and tiny moss-covered shoes. They were FAIRIES! The girl fairy pointed at Mr. Wienie's head and stomped her foot on the floor next to it. A cloud of plum-colored dust rose from where her foot hit the floor. It lingered just long enough in front of his nose; it caused him to sneeze.

I pulled my head back into the tree, turned around as carefully as possible, and started climbing back down. Moments later, I stood with my head stuck out from under the bottom of the tree; I was looking for the three fat sugar-plum fairies. I could only see Mr. Wienie lying on his side, snoring. I put the garland and twinkling lights on top of my nose, flipping them over my head; I darted out from underneath the tree. I hurried to Mr. Wienie's side. He smelled of freshly cooked gingerbread. He even had sticky plum jam that glittered all over his muzzle. "Wake up, Mr. Wienie! You've let those sons of bitches get the best of you." I said as I shook him awake.

Mr. Wienie sneezed, then he coughed. He licked his muzzle and yawned. He looked at me with a guilty look all over his face. Shaking my head, I asked, "Well, did you at least think to ask those assholes their names?"

Mr. Wienie's eyes suddenly grew huge, he opened his mouth to say something, but all that came out was plum-colored sugary dust. He pushed himself away from me, pointing to the Christmas tree behind us. "What is it, brother? Do you want to know why you have plum-colored sugar in your mouth?" I snapped at Mr. Wienie. "Do you want to know what those sons of bitches did to you?" I was mad because he promised not to fall asleep and said he would keep an eye out for Sager.

I turned to see what my brother was looking at behind me. My mouth fell open, and I was speechless. Dozens of tiny gingerbread men were running out of the tree toward us. They were strangely decorated with frosting, and each had three plum-colored gumdrops on its chest. They smelled like newly baked cookies fresh out of the oven. Flying just above their heads were the three fat plum-colored fairies, each carrying a bag with plum-colored dust spilling out of it. They were flying straight at Mr. Wienie and me.

Chapter 2

THE SOUNDS OF CHRISTMAS MUSIC AND THE SMELL OF gingerbread baking woke me from a deep sleep. Quickly I opened my eyes to look around. Mr. Wienie lay just a few feet away from me; he looked like a present with his front and back feet tied together. "Wienie, wake up; we've been taken prisoner." I whispered to my brother, but he didn't open his eyes. "Why are you sleeping? Well, for shit sakes, what is wrong with you?" I whispered a little louder, trying to get up, and that was when I realized I, too, was tied up. I tried to wiggle closer to my brother, thinking maybe I could lick his face to wake him up.

Mr. Wienie's muzzle had more of that sticky, glittery plum jam all over it. He was fast asleep. I watched as his eyes moved back and forth under his eyelids. His tail thumped the floor wildly while his feet moved like he was running. Whatever was in that sticky jam was all over his muzzle and had knocked him out again.

It sent a shiver down my spine, remembering how the gingerbread men came out of the Christmas tree to attack us. The last thing I remember was those fairies throwing plum-colored sugar in my face, knocking me to the ground next to my brother. I thought fairies were supposed to be friendly. I groaned as I struggled to free myself, suddenly realizing we were not in our living room in front of the Christmas tree. We were in the middle of a kitchen with two large ovens; shelves with bags of flour and sugar outlined the room. Two large sinks were piled high with dirty mixing bowls and cookie cutters.

Feeling afraid, looking for a way out, I scanned the room. That's when I noticed the ceiling looked like a glass dome. At the top, red, green, and blue lights flashed continuously as if they were playing a rhythmic tune. Oddly, snow was falling down the outside of the dome. All along the dome's edge stood an army of freshly baked gingerbread men waiting to be frosted and receive their gumdrop buttons.

I tried to wake Mr. Wienie again, but it was no use; he was out. I tried chewing through the shiny ropes that held me captive. "What the hell is this stuff made of?" I said, frustrated because I couldn't chew through it.

Then I heard the same voice I had heard earlier in the Christmas tree, "It's Christmas tinsel, you silly ginger. It's made by the most skilled elves in Santa's workshop, so stop struggling! I will have you set loose in a minute; I have work for you to do, so be quiet, or I will wash your naughty cussing mouth out with soap!"

I swallowed hard as one word came to my mind, soap! Then I thought, damn the soap! I'm not going down without a fight! I started to call her a horse's ass when the fairy held up her hand and said, "Do I need to sprinkle more sugar plum dust on you?"

Dance of The Sugar Plum Wienie

So, I sat quietly as the fat fairy hovered over me, scolding me for cussing. Two more fairies came into the room. It was clear who was in charge as the much bigger girl fairy, who said who name was Martha, began spouting orders. "Maybell, you and Rosco untie our guests and wake up the fat one. I need help in the kitchen. I'm almost out of gingerbread cookie dough."

Before I could resist or struggle, Maybell and Rosco flew over and landed on my feet. Maybell smiled with a weak, impish grin and said, "Please do what my sister says. She has never been this naughty at Christmas time before, and I think she had one too many eggnogs right before we snuck away from Santa's workshop."

Maybell and Rosco used tiny knives to cut the tinsel that held my feet together. It felt good to move my feet. I rolled to my side and sat up. My right hind foot had gone to sleep, which sent tingling feelings up my leg. I watched as the two fat sugar plum fairies went to work on my brother. They cut his feet loose and then tried to wake him up.

First, they poked their fingers into Mr. Wienie's ribs, then tickled the hair between his toes on his back feet. Mr. Wienie kicked his foot, hitting Rosco in the face and sending him to the other side of the room. Giggling, Mr. Wienie rolled over, saying, "Jessica, we barely know each other!" Rosco shot across the room from the force of Mr. Wienie's sleepy kick; it left a thick trail of plum-colored sugar dust behind him.

Martha shook her head and shouted, "Rosco, pay attention, or you'll be back on dish duty."

Maybell continued to poke my brother in the ribs. Mr. Wienie rolled to his back, still giggling, and said, "Jessica, I'd love to have ribs for dinner, will there be bacon and gravy on the side?"

Angry that Mr. Wienie had kicked him in the face, Rosco flew back across the room and landed beside Maybell. His shiny wings reflected the bright Christmas lights that seemed to be hanging outside the glass dome where we were being held against our will. I knew Maybell and Rosco would be unable to wake my brother, so I reached over and shook him. Then I shouted, "Wienie, we're surrounded! I need you to form a plan! Wake up!"

Mr. Wienie kicked his hind foot again and released a long, loud howl that sounded like a battle charge. Half asleep and still dreaming, Mr. Wienie coughed and said in a very sleepy voice, "Jessica, is that mistletoe hanging from your...." Suddenly, Mr. Wienie sat up with a startled look on his face. He yawned and licked at the plum jam on his muzzle. As he looked at Maybell and Rosco, I could tell he remembered what had happened. Springing to his feet, baring his teeth; he told me to get behind him.

Martha, who had been watching the whole time, said, "Listen up! My name is Martha, and my brother and sister are the two over there, Rosco and Maybell. Jessica and Ginger, you are now my prisoners; I've had Maybell and Rosco untie you. You must be good little worker elves, or I will have my army of gingerbread men turn you both into cookie dough."

Looking directly at me, then around the room, Mr. Wienie asked, "Who's Ginger?"

I raised my hand and said, "I guess I'm Ginger, and in case you haven't realized it yet, you're Jessica!" But Jessica was a bacon-wrapped dumpling that my brother always dreams about. If Jessica wasn't actually food, my brother always says she would be his perfect soul mate.

Ready to battle, Mr. Wienie kicked each hind foot, saying, "Elizabeth and I are going home!"

Martha pulled what looked like a small dog whistle from her apron pocket. She put it to her lips and blew so hard that plum-colored sugar popped from the top of her head. The gingerbread men that stood silently around the room turned in unison and began marching in place.

Martha blew the whistle again, and the gingerbread army moved into formation. The floor shook from their marching feet, causing the plum-colored sugar on the floor to waft into the air and slowly drift back to the floor.

"Okay, Martha, we will work in your kitchen and do whatever you want. Just promise to take us home when we are done!" I bravely shouted from behind my brother.

Flying over her freshly baked army of gingerbread men, Martha said, "Maybell, get Jessica started making the gingerbread dough. I know he can cook; I watched him in their big kitchen yesterday. Ginger can do the dishes. I'm going to check the door and make sure Rosco closed it completely."

I started to cry. "Oh, Wienie, where are we? I want to go home."

Maybell fluttered in front of me, smiling; she looked just like a ballerina standing on her toes. Then she floated up to look me in the eyes, cocking her head to the side, she said, "Don't cry, Ginger. Martha will be as good as any Sugar Plum Fairy can be."

I tried to smile back; I thought Maybell was nicer than Martha. Suddenly Maybell pinched my cheek so hard it caused me to cry out, and I flinched from the pain.

"Stop that; what's wrong with you? You're hurting my sister!" Mr. Wienie barked, baring his teeth at the impish little plum-shaped fairy.

"Sugar Plum Fairies are impishly sweet! Especially girl Sugar Plum Fairies, Jessica. It's their way of getting what they want." Rosco said.

Mr. Wienie tried to explain that his name wasn't Jessica, but Rosco ignored him. He turned and motioned for us to follow him. As we walked further into the kitchen, Rosco continued, "My sisters and I have run away from Santa's workshop during Christmas every year since the dark ages. So just play along and do what Martha tells you to do, and none of us will get hurt."

Once we were in the kitchen, Rosco told Mr. Wienie to make more gingerbread dough. He pointed to a mountain of dirty dishes, looked at me, and said, "Ginger, you will wash the dishes."

Rosco explained that I was to wash the mixing bowls and cookie cutters while Mr. Wienie made the Gingerbread dough. Then he handed my brother a tall plum-colored chef's hat. "Back at The North Pole in Santa's kitchen, the elf that wore the tallest hat was in charge of all the baking." Mr. Wienie smiled when he heard Rosco say the words in charge, and he reverently placed the chef's hat on his head. I could see he was very pleased with himself. Knowing how my brother loved to be in charge, rolling my eyes, I groaned, thinking to myself what fresh hell was waiting for me now.

Before I could complain, Rosco held aprons out for us to wear. I asked him where my hat was. Digging around in the apron he was wearing, Rosco pulled out an old dirty red hankey; handing it to me, he said, "Ginger, you can wear my hanky. Years ago, before we started running away from Santa's workshop, Martha always got Maybell and me in so much trouble during Christmas the only thing the head elf would let me wear was this hankey."

Maybell laughed when she heard this; she had been busy flying from shelf to shelf in the kitchen with a clipboard. Quickly she landed beside Rosco, whispering in his ear; she gave him the clipboard and flew away, leaving a trail of plum-colored sugar dust behind her.

Dance of The Sugar Plum Wienie

"Rosco, why would anyone want to run away from Santa's workshop?" I asked as I tied the dirty hankey on my head.

"Well, it's a long story, but I can tell you we ran away because Martha wanted us to. She's more impish than any other Sugar Plum Fairy has ever been. One year long ago, she went with Santa to deliver Christmas presents. It was long before humans wrote stories about Christmas, and she got lost. Santa spent years looking for her, and when Santa finally found her, she was traveling with a ballet company." He flew over to the edge of the sink filled with dirty mixing bowls. Sitting down, looking sad, his wings drooped.

"Oh, Rosco! How sad." I whispered right into Rosco's face. He turned bright purplish pink. Smiling, he tried to kiss me on the cheek. Remembering how Maybell had pinched me earlier, I flinched away.

These Sugar Plum Fairies were hard to read. I could see that they each wanted to be good, but how could they; they were Sugar Plum Fairies. I was learning that fairies were indeed very impish!

Looking at the clipboard, Rosco said, "We have to get another two dozen gingerbread men baked and decorated before Martha performs her ballet of Swan Lake." Then he pointed to each shelf containing the unique ingredients to make their gingerbread dough.

I could tell Rosco wasn't paying attention to us or even where he was flying; he bumped into a shelf every now and then, causing flour, sugar, or baking soda to spill onto the floor in front of us as we walked behind him.

"Do you smell that, Wienie? It's cinnamon and nutmeg and something else." I whispered.

"Cloves Elizabeth, it's for the eggnog that Maybell told us her sister, Martha, drinks. It's also loaded with rum. I could smell it on

Martha's breath when she was talking to us." Mr. Wienie whispered back.

"Wienie, I should have stayed out of our Christmas tree. I bet Sager is worried about us; she probably thinks you and I are outside playing in the snow. Before breakfast this morning, she caught me in the tree and told me if I must play around trees, I was supposed to have you take me outside. How will she know where to look for us now?"

"I agree, Elizabeth; I wonder how we will find our home if we don't know where we are." Mr. Wienie stopped, then said, "Let's just do what the fat fairies want, and I'll take care of the rest." Mr. Wienie sounded so official; I was beginning to think he was secretly enjoying this, especially after Rosco made him the 'head' chef of the kitchen.

"Hey, no talking!" Maybell scolded as she landed in front of us. Not only were these fairies impish, but they were sneaky as well.

"Martha doesn't like her elves talking while they are supposed to be working," Maybell said as she shook her finger at Rosco, who was oblivious that my brother and I were not even listening to him. "Rosco, you need to get Jessica and Ginger busy. When Martha comes back, and we have no gingerbread cookies made, and these dishes are still dirty, she'll make us help them." Maybell said, flying over the sink of dishes. "I still need to get the theater ready for the ballet."

Her voice was tiny and almost irritating as she continued shaking her finger at Rosco. "Ginger is stalling, and she's only asking questions to distract you," then she grabbed Rosco by his pointy ear and flew away to the other side of the room.

Mr. Wienie and I watched as Rosco and Maybell argued. Even though they were fairies, they quarreled just like Sager and Mr.

Wienie. Before they both flew away, Rosco told us that Martha might let us watch the ballet if we were good and only if the gingerbread dough was made and I finished the dishes. Maybell looked wistful when she said, "This year, the ballet is going to be the best one yet. So, stop talking and be good little worker elves, or I just might have to pinch your cheek." I flinched away as she reached out, trying to pinch me again.

Chapter 3

I STOOD IN FRONT OF THE SINK, OVERWHELMED BY ALL the dirty mixing bowls and cookie cutters, hating Christmas and cookies. Frustrated, I jerked the hankey off my head and tied it around my neck. Mr. Wienie hummed happily behind me as he came over to pile more mixing bowls and utensils on the counter beside me.

"Wienie, why are you humming?" I shouted, emptying the sink to make fresh dishwater.

"Do the dishes, Elizabeth; stop making waves." My brother replied to me.

Turning back to the sink, I mocked him by repeating what he had just said. "Do the dishes, Elizabeth." Then I said, "Well, damn, if they think I'm going to be happy about cleaning, they can kiss my Christmas ass." I grabbed the dishcloth and started working.

Mr. Wienie was almost finished mixing the gingerbread dough when he snuck over to the eggnog fountain and filled a huge measuring cup full. He returned to the bowl of dough, poured it in, and mixed it up. After licking his paws clean, he added more vanilla and a whole handful of cinnamon. I had almost finished washing all of the dishes when my brother piled more dirty mixing bowls beside me on the counter. I yelled, "Damn it, Wienie!" I spun around to show him my paws, saying, "Look at my beautiful Christmas polish. It's ruined; look at my pads; they are all wrinkly."

Mr. Wienie wobbled back and forth before me, saying, "Ginger, you're doing a great job."

I leaned close to his muzzle and sniffed. "Why do you smell like cloves and rum?" I said as I pulled my head back and waved my paw in front of my face. "Have you been sampling Martha's eggnog?" I asked.

Mr. Wienie hiccupped and staggered back to the counter where all the cookie cutters lay, but before he started to roll out more dough, he said, "I'm a victim of circumstance Elizabeth."

We were almost finished; we needed to bake a few more cookies, finish the rest of the dishes, and hopefully, Martha would just set us free. I rushed about the kitchen, putting away the dishes I had just washed, when Martha burst into the room, blowing her whistle.

The sound was sharp and made my ears ring. I dropped a huge glass bowl on the floor; it shattered into a million pieces. "It smells delicious in here, my busy little elves. I have decided to keep you both and never let either one of you go home." Martha sang.

I growled at her and barked, "You can kiss a big ole goose's ass if you think my brother and I will stay here with you! I want to go home, and I promise you if you don't let us go when my big sister finds us, she'll kick the shit out of you and your army of gingerbread men."

With a devilish smile, Martha said, "Oh really? Let me show you something, Ginger, and you too, Jessica."

Dance of The Sugar Plum Wienie

Then she blew her tiny whistle again. The floor began to shake as twelve of Martha's gingerbread men marched two by two into the kitchen; as the last four rounded the corner, I could see they were carrying something that looked like a Christmas gift which they sat at my feet.

As she flew over to have a cup of eggnog, Martha demanded, "Maybell, show our newest guest where she'll be staying. I want Rosco to take Jessica and Ginger to help him prepare the ballet stage for me to perform Swan Lake."

Howling, I realized it was Sager. I yelled, "Martha, cut our sister loose right now!" The gingerbread men had her gagged and tied up.

"No one is to untie our newest elf," Martha said to Maybell and Rosco, tapping her whistle in the palm of her tiny sugar plum hand. "This one can't be trusted; she has destroyed a dozen of my gingerbread men, tearing them in half! She has bitten seven of my gingerbread men standing here; plus, she has torn a hole in the arm of my outfit. I planned on wearing it for tonight's ballet performance." Martha announced, holding her arm up to show us where Sager had bitten her. "What's her name anyway? I'd like to know before I have my army of gingerbread men turn her into cookie dough." Martha asked and then laughed as she said, "Maybe I will name the cookies after her!"

I howled as loud as possible, and colorful cuss words flew from my mouth. I hadn't even realized I was crying until Rosco landed on my back, patting my head, saying, "Don't cry, Ginger."

Martha reached for her cup but discovered Mr. Wienie was holding it. He had just filled it with eggnog, holding the cup out for her to take; she was unsure if she wanted it. Mr. Wienie lifted the cup he had been drinking from and said, "Congratulations!"

It was hard to tell if Martha was happy or mad as she moved closer to him. She looked at Mr. Wienie from head to toe; as though she was sizing him up for a suit of clothes. Then she asked him, "Congratulations for what, Jessica?"

Mr. Wienie took the cup he had been holding for Martha and thrust into her hand, then took the cup he had been drinking from, dipped it entirely into the eggnog, and said, "It's been a while since my sisters and I have had a worthy opponent! When declaring war, you should always know your enemy." Mr. Wienie drank all the eggnog in the cup. Then he dipped his cup again into the eggnog, raised it as if to toast Martha, and said, "My name is Mr. Wienie, not Jessica! This cussing little red doxie over here is a Ginger, but her name is Elizabeth James! Your newest elf there on the floor is Sager Jane, aka the babysitter, and if you know anything about babysitters...."

Interrupting my brother, I shouted, "They don't take shit from anyone!"

Martha blew her whistle again and yelled, "Rosco, take Jessica and Ginger to the theater. Tie up Ginger; she needs her mouth washed out with soap as soon as the ballet is over. Get Jessica into a costume; I want him to dance Swan Lake with me."

The dressing room Rosco led my brother and me to was nothing more than an old storage room that smelled sour from old wet rags left in a mop bucket. There was a long mirror on the wall, with a small stool beside it, and on the far wall were two small lockers with Rosco and Maybell's names on them. Rosco pulled a green piece of paper from his apron and handed it to me.

I scanned the paper; it was a to-do list; not only was I doing the dishes again, but I had to clean the bathrooms, mop all the floors, and then report to Martha so she could wash my mouth out with soap. As I read to the bottom, I couldn't help myself; I loudly said, "Oh, F**k," out loud!

"What did you say?" Rosco asked me.

I looked at Mr. Wienie, nodding my head so he would agree with me, and said, "Fudge, I said fudge, right Wienie." Then I laughed, looking at Rosco, and said, "You know Rosco... fudge. Marshmallows and chocolate! Oh, fuddddgggee, I sure wish I had some hot chocolate!" I said, laughing trying to convince him I hadn't cussed.

Rosco smiled impishly, saying, "That's what we Sugar Plum Fairies love about you, Ginger. You're so naughty, yet everyone thinks you are innocent, and I can tell that even Martha loves that about you! You would make a great Sugar Plum Fairy, but you are an elf, and elves do not cuss! They only work and do as they are told! The sooner you learn that and stop with your potty mouth, the better your life here will be."

Rosco opened the locker door with his name on it and began digging around at the bottom. Trying to think of ways to prolong the inevitable mouth washing I knew was coming, I asked him what Martha loved about Mr. Wienie.

Rosco stood up, leaning against the door; he relaxed and smiled at Mr. Wienie, saying, "Martha also loves that Jessica here only thinks about what he wants. You both are all the wonderful things that Christmas is always about. Being naughty and still getting what you want!"

Hoping to keep him distracted, I said, "Rosco, you never finished telling us why every year Martha makes you and Maybell run away with her from Santa's workshop."

I could tell Rosco was enjoying himself as he began to explain, "To truly understand who and what Sugar Plum Fairies are, you first need to know where we come from. Long ago, the spirit of Christmas made the first Sugar Plum Fairies appear. We are the sugar plums dancing in your head on a cold winter's night. We hold the memories of Christmas past, keeping the spirit alive year after year. You see, Ginger, we are not all bad. But we are fairies, and fairies must be impishly sweet sometimes. Over the years, Santa's coat and boots have become covered in our dust; this is what keeps him so jolly. Santa even uses our sugar dust to make his reindeer fly."

"But Rosco, why do all three of you leave Santa's workshop every year?" I asked again.

"I told you earlier, Ginger, that one year Martha got to go with Santa on Christmas Eve to deliver all the presents. The year was 1892, the first time Santa delivered gifts to all the children in Paris. It's never been said how or why Martha got lost, but Santa spent years looking for her. When he finally found her, she was in America. She had fallen in love with a Sugar Plum Fairy named Valentino. They had been dancing and traveling with a ballet company. When Martha has too much eggnog, she will admit it was the happiest time of her life. When Santa found Martha, he made her return with him to the North Pole. Martha never got the chance to tell Valentino she loved him. Santa promised her he would find Valentino. Maybell and I have also looked for him for years. Martha is brokenhearted; this is why she makes us sneak away from Santa's workshop every Christmas, hoping to find Valentino. She wants to bring him to the North Pole to live with us."

Suddenly Rosco snapped at me; he realized I had been inching my way toward the door. "Now, be still, Ginger; I'm done with your stalling questions. I need to get Jessica ready for his part in the ballet."

I wanted to run away from him and find Sager; Mr. Wienie was in no shape at all to run. He had one too many of Marth's eggnog drinks, and I wondered how he could perform the ballet; I swear he looked like he needed a nap.

As Rosco turned back to the locker and continued looking for a costume for Mr. Wienie, I said, "Where is Martha's dressing room? This isn't at all what I thought a dressing room would look like."

Rosco answered, "Martha has the nicest dressing room just across the hallway; she's the star of our ballet."

Rosco finally found plum-colored tights with a white leotard and matching ballet shoes. He tossed the outfit in front of Mr. Wienie and told him to get dressed. Then he opened the door to the storage room and stepped into the hallway closing the door behind him. A few seconds later, he opened the door and said, "Jessica, you need to get ready; I'll be back in a minute. Ginger, you need to follow me to the theater."

I followed Rosco to the theater, where he led me to the front row, telling me to stay here. Once he walked away, I climbed to the back of the seat, searching the theater for Sager. I spotted her just a few rows above me; she was still gagged and tied up. At the back of the theater, twelve gingerbread men stood guard.

I started to go to Sager, but the lights dimmed as the curtain rose. Music began playing as Martha stood center stage in a plum-colored tutu. Swaying back and forth, she began to dance, jumping high into the air and twirling around the stage to the soft sound of ballet music.

Landing gracefully, she twirled across the stage and held her hands as if waiting for her true love to appear. Mr. Wienie leaped onto the stage; I watched as he scanned the theater each time he bowed to the audience. I knew he was looking for Sager and me.

Mr. Wienie stood on his hind legs, raised his front legs above his head, and twirled across the stage. Martha was still standing with her arms open, waiting for Mr. Wienie to lift her into the air. He spun as fast as he could around Martha and grabbed her tutu, but before slinging her to the other side of the stage, he shook her. On the opposite side of the stage, Martha struggled to land on her feet. It was apparent Mr. Wienie shook her really hard because plum-colored sugar dust hung in the air above his head. I could tell my brother was still a little drunk from all the eggnog he had earlier. I quickly glanced at Sager; she had removed her gag and was chewing the tinsel that bound her feet.

The soft music changed tempo as Martha flitted her way around the stage again, pretending to still look for her one true love. She jumped excitedly into the air, landing in front of Mr. Wienie as if she had suddenly found him. Martha raised her arms again, waiting to be lifted into the air, but Mr. Wienie gracefully danced away from her, leaping into the air as if he hadn't seen her. He was searching for the one he longed for. Who knew my brother could dance so well, it was like he was born for the lights of the stage.

The music became louder; it was obvious that a crucial part of the ballet was about to happen. Holding her arms above her head, Martha chased Mr. Wienie from one side of the stage to the other, wanting to be lifted into the air. I could see that my brother was enjoying this great game of chase, and I wondered what battle plan he was putting into action.

Every time Martha was close enough for Mr. Wienie to touch her, he would shake and sling her to the opposite side of the stage. The stage was covered entirely with plum-colored sugar dust, making Mr. Wienie look like he was flying. Martha was enraged; she wanted to be raised in the air like a beautiful white swan. That's when Sager slipped into the seat next to me. Quickly she covered my mouth, so I wouldn't scream, then she pointed behind her. When I looked, all twelve gingerbread men lay in a pile of dust. I giggled at the thought of Sager quietly tearing up each gingerbread man. She whispered to me to be still; she knew our brother would let us know when it was time to take out Martha and her siblings.

Maybell and Rosco worked furiously behind the scenes changing the scenery each time the curtain dropped. Sager and I watched on as Mr. Wienie and Martha danced to the music of the tragic story of Swan Lake. Martha's tutu hung askew on her hips as she picked herself up from the floor from Mr. Wienie, shaking her for the fifth or sixth time. I enjoyed watching Martha get what was coming to her, and I giggled because I had lost count of how many times my brother threw her across the stage.

Instead of gracefully flitting across the stage, Martha flew at Mr. Wienie this time; it was clear that he had overplayed his hand. Mr. Wienie bowed and said, "Sager, Elizabeth, is that a fat lady I hear singing?" Then he kicked each hind foot and raised his head to howl. Sager grabbed me, and we raced to the stage, ready for battle. Mr. Wienie lept into the air and landed on top of Martha just as Sager and I made it onto the stage. Mr. Wienie had Martha pinned on her back; when he wasn't biting her, he was yelling in her face. Sager told me to help our brother, and she would take care of Maybell and Rosco. They smiled impishly at each other as they watched Mr. Wienie and Martha rolling around, fighting on the floor. Sager growled as we approached; the hair on the back of her neck was raised. She was ready to finish this fight so we could go home.

I started laughing because I realized we were all just standing there watching Mr. Wienie and Martha fighting. It was like a strange after-school special on tv, where the underdog was tired of being bullied.

Martha was screaming for her siblings to help her, and Mr. Wienie asked her if she was ready to make her debut; then, he grasped her around the neck and jumped over our heads. I watched as my brother flew over my head, shaking Martha hard again, landing center stage with Martha still in his mouth; he hoisted her high in the air and slammed her to the floor. Then he bowed to each side of the stage.

We all thought ole Martha was passed out, but when Mr. Wienie turned to look at Martha again, she was sitting with her whistle in her mouth. Before she could blow into the whistle, I laughed and said, "No need to call for your army of gingerbread men, you old bitch; my sister turned them all to dust."

Martha's wings fluttered fast as she flew at me. Sager jumped in the air and kicked just as she was about to attack. The fight was on again, only this time, Maybell and Rosco helped their sister. Martha chased me around the stage, telling me she couldn't wait to wash out my nasty mouth. She kept reminding me that I was one of her elves, and her elves did not cuss!

Martha finally stopped chasing me because she could see that Mr. Wienie had Rosco pinned down, and Sager had grabbed Maybell out of the air. It was over; Martha hovered just above our heads; I told her we had won and that no one else would get hurt if she let us go home.

Martha laughed as she said, "Who's going home? You are home already!" Then she blew hard into the whistle and finished saying, "You stupid Ginger, a baker's dozen has thirteen cookies." The last gingerbread man climbed to the stage. With every step, the stage floor shook, knocking me off my feet.

The plum-colored sugar dust that covered the floor lofted high into the air, and it was hard to see. Martha flew at Mr. Wienie and hit him in the face with a handful of plum colored-sugar dust, but before Mr. Wienie could snatch her out of the air, he passed out on top of Rosco. Sager yelled for me to run just as Martha knocked her out too.

I panicked and started running; I could hear Martha telling Maybell to mix Sager and Mr. Wienie into the gingerbread dough, then she told Rosco to go to the kitchen and get a brush and soap ready. I was so afraid that I didn't even see that I was running right into the arms of Martha's thirteenth gingerbread man. He picked me up and started toward the kitchen. Martha laughed as she called for Rosco and asked him, "Where's the eggnog? I need a drink before I wash Ginger's nasty mouth out."

I bit at the gingerbread man, and he slung me over his shoulder like a sack of flour. "Wienie…. Sager…" I screamed, but it was no use; they were both out and already dreaming.

In the kitchen, the gingerbread man held me hostage until Rosco showed up. I tried to get Rosco to talk to me, but he was busy finding the brush Martha requested to wash my mouth out with. I could hear Martha screaming for Maybell in the hallway. As she approached, Rosco laid the brush beside me on the floor, along with a bar of green soap; the fresh scent of Irish Spring filled my nose.

Martha flew through the doors with Maybell behind her, she went straight to the eggnog, but before having a drink, she scolded Rosco by saying, "I told you to bring me a drink. Do I have to wash your mouth out as well?"

Rosco told me to be still and get ready to open my mouth. Martha picked up the brush Rosco had just laid beside me; inspecting it, I cringed as I watched her scrubbing it back and forth across the palm of her hand. Satisfied with the brush, she placed it back on the floor beside me. Martha asked me, putting her hands on her hips, "Ginger, do you have any final nasty words before I wash out your mouth?"

This was it; here it comes, soap poisoning; it would be just like the kid in that Christmas story movie; nothing would taste right ever again. I searched the room, still looking for my sister and brother.

Martha handed the brush to Maybell, told her to soap it up, and demanded that I open my mouth. Tears sprang to my eyes, and I realized we would never see home again. I knew I should have listened to Sager and stayed out from under our Christmas tree, and then I asked, "Where are my siblings?" Martha didn't answer my question; Rosco tried to force my mouth open, and I shook my head. I laid down and covered my head with my paws, promising never to cuss again. The room was quiet, and I couldn't smell soap anymore. I lay as still as possible, hoping that my promise had changed their minds. I wanted to peek to see what was going on. Suddenly I was lifted into the air and then placed back onto the floor. I was afraid to open my eyes, but something was different; the floor was warm, and I could smell pinecones. I looked up and saw that Sager, Mr. Wienie, and I were on the floor beside our Christmas tree; we were home. Sager and Mr. Wienie were still tied together with tinsel.

I saw Santa Claus, with a big smile standing behind Sager and Mr. Wienie. He touched the tinsel that held them tied together, making it disappear before hitting the floor. My sister wagged her tail, and Mr. Wienie said, "Thanks, Santa, I always knew you were real."

Santa Claus looked just like all the Christmas stories had described, except that his coat and shiny black boots were covered in sugar plum dust. He bent down to one knee and rubbed each of us behind our ears. "Oh, Santa! I love you," I said, jumping to lick his face. Sager and Mr. Wienie both climbed into Santa's lap, and before Santa knew it, he was sitting on the floor, holding all three of us. Hugging us, Santa laughed, then kissed the tops of our heads; that's when I smelled gingerbread cookies. Whining, I froze and dug my head into Santa's coat, trying to hide, saying, "Santa, hide me; Martha is coming to get me again."

Santa Claus let out a long Ho Ho Ho Ho and reached for an ornament lying on the floor beside our Christmas Tree. He held it up and explained that we had never left home. Martha and her gingerbread men had trapped us inside an enchanted Christmas ornament. As he got to his feet, he said, "No need to worry about Martha any longer, Elizabeth. I am late getting here tonight because I found Valentino; he is waiting for Martha in the sleigh."

I felt so sleepy as Santa tucked each of us into our beds; we were finally safe in our home. He kissed each of us on the head, telling us to go to sleep; there would be presents to open in the morning. Both Sager and Mr. Wienie closed their eyes. I sat up because Santa handed me a present before leaving. Setting the gift on my pillow, I wiggled out of bed to see Santa Claus disappearing up the chimney. Then I rushed back to my bed, wondering what was in the package. I held the Christmas gift from Santa tightly to my chest, then I gently unwrapped my gift and whispered, "Santa Claus really does see and hear us." My gift from Santa Claus was Martha's bar of soap, and I said, "Son of a Bitch." In the distance, I heard Santa Claus say, "Merry Christmas to all. And to all, a good night."

The End.

Pepper Ann (Cendy's Kitty)

Albert and The Glass Figurine

Written By:

Wendy J. Hatfield

Chapter 1

PAULA HUMMED EXCITEDLY AS SHE RUSHED AROUND the house, packing her bags for what promised to be a wonderful and relaxing vacation. She told Mishka and me to watch for the taxi that should be arriving any minute. She reminded us that she posted our eating schedule along with the house rules and emergency numbers on the frig. She told us no begging for extra treats once her sister arrived.

Then she said, "Manhattan, please, try to keep your brother, Mishka, out of trouble; you know how he can be." Even though she was smiling, she sounded slightly worried. Paula, my human mother, usually calls me Manny, but this time she called me Manhattan. When Paula uses our full names, we know she means business.

Mishka looked at Paula, then at me, and acted as if he had no idea what she was referring to. He flexed his paw, exposing his nails, then yawned, and with a swish of his tail, he slunk out of the room.

My brother is famous for being utterly oblivious to his own actions and anything else going on in a room. I guess Paula named him right; when she brought him home from the Elks Lodge, she said his name was Mishka, but later she admitted that it was supposed to be Mischief. Besides, black cats are always full of mischief.

At the time, we all laughed because when Paula comes home every night from the Elks Lodge, she is very rosy-cheeked and always walks and talks funny.

Paula says she named me after her second favorite beverage. She says this because she considered naming me after her first favorite. She thought better of it because she refused to call me indoors from outside by yelling for Bloody Mary! Not to mention the fact that I'm a gray boy cat.

Paula emerged from her room carrying her suitcases just as the taxi arrived and honked. A short bald man wearing a uniform knocked on the door as she opened it; he smiled and asked her if she was ready to go. She nodded her head yes and handed the man her suitcases. She stepped onto the porch and turned toward us, saying, "Now you two be good kitties, stay in the house, no fighting, and don't break anything. You know I love you both." Then she closed the door.

We both watched from our favorite seat in the window as the taxicab disappeared down the road. Right on cue, with his tail mischievously waving in the air, Mishka looked at me and said, "Where's the catnip?"

"Oh no, you don't." I snapped back at him, "Remember the last time we had catnip? We were playing in Paula's bedroom, and I ended up knocking over her perfume bottles and breaking some of them. I had a heck of a time hiding all the broken glass from her."

Albert and The Glass Figurine

Protesting, Mishka said, "What's wrong with you? Come on, that night was a blast!" My brother said it with so much enthusiasm that I almost gave in. Then he said, "Manny, you really caught some air with that jump, and as for the curtains, well, that was too funny!" Mishka stood on his hind feet with his front paws out to the side, saying, "You looked like you were surfing them all the way from the ceiling to the floor!"

Thank goodness Paula came home a bit later than usual from the Elks Lodge. While she was gone, we had gotten into the catnip and decided to play double-dog dare-ya. It's what we call our go-to catnip game.

That night Mishka dared me to jump from Paula's bed to the dresser, then to the windowsill, and then back to the top of the dresser, all without stopping. I could have made it if I hadn't had that extra bite of catnip! It really was a night for the record books!

I misjudged the jump back to the dresser and ended up grabbing the curtains, and the rest is history. However, that night I scored significant points for catching the most air. I always win big when we play games, especially when it comes to double-dog dare-ya mixed with a bit of catnip.

Mishka jumped down from the window and rubbed his whiskers against the leg of Paula's chair. He licked his front paw, arched his back, then stretched and flexed his toenails; he clawed his way to the top of the chair. He jumped from the top of her chair to the back of the sofa, yowling; he said, "You do realize this vacation of ours is going to be so dull because of all Paula's rules." He then mumbled something indecipherable under his breath. I could swear I heard him say Paula wouldn't be gone long enough, and I am always captain no-fun.

When Mishka was just a kitten, he was so sweet, innocent, and energetic. He really loves to play and get into mischief fully living up to his actual name. Now that I think about it, my brother has always referred to me as captain no fun. With Paula being away yet again, I figured it would be an excellent time to bond with my brother. I was content, knowing we could just hang out, watch television, and have snacks.

After a quick nap, Mishka sat looking out the big window watching the birds and squirrels fighting over a feeder that hung from one of the trees in the front yard. His tail and whiskers twitched from side to side, and his feet slowly moved up and down. Then he attacks, but the window reminds him that he is never going to catch those birds and squirrels!

Mishka asked me if I thought squirrels or birds could talk and why the squirrels were so selfish with food. I told him I wasn't sure because I had never spoken to anyone other than him. I could tell my brother was bored again and becoming agitated. I knew I needed to do something to distract his attention away from the window.

I suggested we play a game, and after naming a long list, he finally agreed to a game of Yahtzee with me. Then he asked if I wanted to share a can of tuna while we played. We played most of the day; Mishka kept a record of who won and who lost. I'm always the winner when we play any game, except for this day. This day I let my little brother win to keep his attention away from the window and his spirits high. Gloating after every game he won, he drew a giant winner's circle around his name.

Throughout the day, I occasionally glanced through the window when suddenly, a movement caught my eye. Despite myself, my attention was riveted to the window. I noticed there were two squirrels perched high in a tree, watching us as we played. To my dismay, Mishka asked what I found so fascinating out the window; he couldn't stand himself; he needed to have a peek at what I was seeing. He was so curious that he left the game he was winning. From the way his ears flattened out, I could tell that he had spotted the two squirrels I saw.

I ran to the window and stood beside Mishka just in time to see that the two squirrels were making their way at a fast pace down the tree trunk. Before they reached the ground, one of the squirrels surprised Mishka by jumping toward the window, which caused him to jump backward. He landed on the edge of the sofa table; instantly, he pushed off it jumping back to the window, causing the table to rock back and forth. I raced to grab the lamp before it crashed to the floor; instead, I managed to knock over a glass figurine that was also on the table.

Mishka let out an excited yowl and tried to high-five me, saying, "Wow, good catch, brother, you really caught some air with that jump!"

I did want to celebrate the air I caught with that jump, but after seeing the broken figurine pieces that now lay at my feet, I could only stand there wondering how we would put this one back together. Mishka must have thought that I didn't see his high five, so he did it again and said, "Don't leave a brother hanging, especially after that gnarly jump!"

Scolding my brother, I explained that there was no way to fix this. I told him this figurine was not just chipped; it was shattered into a million tiny pieces. Then I asked him, "How will we ever put this one back together?" I tried to calm myself down before saying something I might regret later."

Mishka suggested we buy a new one or get something else to replace it with. He was picking up the pieces when he found one with a label on it; he said, "It looks like Paula bought this at the Bison Ranch."

Shaking my head, knowing I wouldn't receive a decent answer, I asked him, "Where do you think this place might be, and how do you suggest we get there?"

Taking me at my word, Mishka threw his front paws in the air, saying, "I don't know." Then he threw me two victorious thumbs up and gleefully continued saying, "Maybe we could call an Uber. You know, those people that bring Paula home when she's been at the Elks Lodge for too long."

We heard scratching noises outside the front door. Eager to be the first to escape our current issue, Mishka launched himself from a seated position over my head; getting to the door before me, he opened it, and to our surprise, the two squirrels were sitting at Paula's tiny table on the porch.

"Squirrels!" Mishka said, "This is gonna be fun!" He crouched down as his tail swished from side to side. I could tell he was judging the distance to jump in the middle of the table. I slammed the door closed as he jumped; he hit the door with a loud thud and slid to the floor. Rubbing his head, my brother yelled, "Hey, why did you do that? I was going to scare the crap out of them; after all, it's their fault you broke the figurine."

A million things that could have gone wrong rushed through my mind. What if my brother was to attack them and got hurt, or even worse, he got lost? That's why I quickly closed the door. Outside we could hear the squirrels chattering back and forth; they were laughing at us! Mishka, now enraged, jerked the door open and screamed, "What are you two laughing at, and why are you on our porch?

Because of you two, Manny has now broken one of the house rules! My head hurts, and we need to find a Bison Ranch!"

The two squirrels continued to laugh, pointing at Mishka while mimicking him with their tails. He prepared to lunge at them when suddenly, a small bird landed in front of us. The little bird waved its wings in front of Mishka's face saying, "It's no use arguing with them; you can't reason with a squirrel."

Shocked that this bird spoke to us, arching his back, Mishka jumped backward, hissing loudly, "Manny, they can talk."

The little bird sang its words; it was hard to understand at first, and we were speechless, to say the least. The little bird continued to explain how squirrels act and why it was best to just ignore them.

Mishka prepared himself to attack the squirrels again because they were now mimicking the little bird. I reached down and held onto his tail, still trying to understand what the little bird was saying.

Completely frustrated with the little bird and the squirrels, Mishka pulled his tail away from my paw. He shouted, "We have a crisis going on right now; I repeat, we have a crisis! My brother has broken a house rule, and unless you know where a Bison Ranch is and how we can get there, then please tell us. Otherwise, take these two crazy squirrels and fly away."

I waited for the bird to stop talking and singing; when it did, I asked if it knew how we could get to a Bison Ranch. The bird started singing, telling me her name was Sally and that she knew the way to the Bison Ranch, but that was only because she could fly. She said if we could fly, she would show us and then sang some more.

Mishka blurted, "Can you just tell us without all the extra fluff! My brother and I have a lot to think about right now; he just broke a rule!"

Then he went back to contemplating attacking the two squirrels; he hadn't noticed a group of rabbits approaching the bottom of the staircase. I started to interrupt, except the little bird said, "Bison Ranch, I know where that is. I even know some of the animals that live there. They have all kinds of animals." The little bird turned in the direction of the rabbits, bringing them to Mishka's attention, then flew away.

One of the rabbits said, "I'm Jack, and I know how you can get to the Bison Ranch; we are going there tomorrow. In fact, if you meet us at the end of this road on the corner around noon tomorrow, the both of you can go with us!"

Mishka looked surprised, and I was impressed that he just sat down, exhausted from listening to the little bird drone on. Feeling a little overwhelmed and needing a moment to think, I pulled my brother into the house and closed the door.

Mishka and I sat in silence for the remainder of the day. It wasn't until I headed to Paula's room with Mishka following me to get ready for bed that he said, "Can you believe all those animals outside can talk! Should we trust that rabbit who said his name was Jack to know where we need to go? What is happening at noon tomorrow that could possibly help us?"

Deep in thought, I told Mishka we would just have to wait and see. "So, we're going then, right?" Mishka asked as he washed his face with his paw; then he yawned and said, "Once we get there, how and where do we get another buffalo figurine?"

"What could it hurt? We might as well try. Go to sleep, Mishka; we will see what happens tomorrow." I said as I wondered how we would make this right; then I thought maybe we should just replace it with something else from around the house.

Chapter 2

THE FOLLOWING DAY WHILE WE ATE BREAKFAST, I LAID down a few rules for Mishka before leaving the house. This would be his first time going past the front porch without being in his pet carrier. I knew this could be a dangerous trip, and we needed to keep our heads about us. Knowing how easy it was for my brother to get sidetracked, I told him I was in charge, so he needed to listen and be close to me at all times. He wasn't too happy about that, but he did agree to listen to everything I said.

As we approached the corner where the rabbit said they would be, a crowd of people stood waving and cheering. I could see old buggies being pulled by horses. Walking up beside us, Jack said, "So, you two are going to go with us after all."

Mishka asked Jack how we were getting to the Bison Ranch. Jack replied with a grin, and before he took off running, he said, "Follow me."

Mishka and I ran as fast as we could, following Jack through the tall grass that opened up into an old parking lot. Jack stopped just short still in the grass, where we could see three more buggies getting ready to enter the parade. Pointing to the last buggy in line, Jack said, "When I say go, we will jump in that one and hide; this parade is headed straight to the Bison Ranch."

Mishka and I were breathing hard; we weren't used to running at such a fast pace for a long distance. Excited, Mishka said, "Manny, wow, we are going to be in a parade today!"

Jack announced it was time to go, and we ran toward the last buggy. Jack was the first one in, then Mishka and me. We had made it, quickly hiding under one of the seats. As the buggy left the empty parking lot and entered the parade, I could hear the crowd that lined both sides of the street cheering. If all went well, soon we would be at our destination; I hoped.

Once we got there, Jack told us to wait until the passengers got off, and then he said I will meet you in the field across from the gift shop. Feeling a little tired, I told Mishka to wake me when we arrived. When he didn't answer, I realized he wasn't beside me; Mishka had crawled out from under the seat and was sitting on the side of the buggy, looking, and waving to the crowds. That's when I saw a woman pick my brother up saying, "Oh, look at this cute little kitty; how did you get in here?"

Then I heard a little boy scream, "I want a kitty!" The seat we were hiding under started to move around, and a chubby little boy's face appeared in front of me; he squealed, saying, "There's another one; there are two kitties!" He pulled on my tail screaming and demanding, "I want them both!"

I ran out from under the seat, and the lady grabbed me. The little boy was now screaming and stomping his feet, demanding that he wanted to hold a kitty, too, so she handed me to him.

I soon learned the little boy's name was Albert because the lady holding my brother asked Albert to sit down four or five times. Mishka was excited because he could see the crowd now, and the lady holding him was cuddling and stroking his chin. Every so often, she would hold up his front paw to wave to the crowds. Mishka was having a great time soaking up all the affection. He was excited to see all the sights as the horses continued to pull the buggies through town.

As we passed through town, Albert's mother pointed to the Elks Lodge and said to him, "Look, honey, that's where my friend Paula and I go to breakfast sometimes. Remember that place? It's where all the big elk heads hang."

Squeezing me extra tight to his side, Albert jumped up, squealing loudly in my ear, demanding, "I want an elk head!" When he sat back down, I was fully aware he was on my tail. Knowing we needed to make it to the Bison Ranch, I resisted the urge to claw him and endured the pain. Then Albert's mother said, "Oh, look, there's Janice's house! That's Paula's sister. She lives right there." The little boy didn't jump and scream this time as he was focused on hugging and squeezing me while running my fur backward. The lady beamed a sweet smile at the child and said, "Now, be nice to the kitty."

Purring and yelling over the crowd, Mishka rubbed his head next to mine, saying, "I'm having a great time," and added, "can you believe we are riding with one of Paula's friends?" Then he gave me the thumbs up!

The crowds were thinning out, and I could tell we were leaving town; maybe we were getting closer to the Bison Ranch. I hoped so because I was tired of Albert and the way he was holding me. Albert's mother became overly excited and called him by name, pointing, she said. "Albert, stand up quick; look over there; it's antelope."

The little boy jumped to his feet, and I flew forward, causing him to drop me and catch me upside down. He stood there jumping in place as I struggled to turn myself right side up. I reached over and whispered to Mishka, "Remember the rules we discussed? I'm going to get you when we get home!"

Mishka couldn't hear me over the excitement in Albert's voice. He thought I was having fun being bounced around like a toy. Mishka leaned over and yelled to me, "Hey, you're missing out on all the fun of this parade! Look at that; it's antelope! Wow, I'll never forget this day, Manny! Good thing you broke the figurine! Stop playing around with Albert and take in the sights." Then he nuzzled Albert's mother with his head, and as she cuddled him, he gave me the thumbs up again!

Finally, we approached a sign that read, 'Welcome to the Bison Ranch.' I looked in the direction of our hiding place in the buggy and saw that Jack, the rabbit, had been watching us. He laughed and then put up his paw as if to say, just hold on; we are almost there. I tried to get Mishka's attention to tell him that we had arrived, but he had crawled inside Albert's mother's coat to take a nap.

All the buggies came to a stop, and the passengers were exiting. Albert's mother told him to gather his things and not to lose his new kitty. At that moment, I felt afraid and nauseous. How were we going to get away from these people? Mishka had stopped listening to me and was enjoying all the attention being lavished on him at the moment.

Calling over her shoulder, Albert's mother said, "Come on, Albert, I will get you an ice cream, and I want to go to the gift shop." That's when Albert squealed loudly, dropping me.

Once my feet hit the ground, I ran as fast as possible toward the field. I looked back, thinking Mishka might be following me, but he wasn't. He was still napping in Albert's mother's coat. The last thing I saw was Albert screaming and following his mother into the gift shop.

As I approached, Jack held back the tall grass so I could see where he was standing. He said, "They still have your brother."

Upset and afraid, I held my head as I sat down. Wishing we hadn't come here and feeling angry that Mishka wouldn't listen to me. Jack asked me why we needed to come to the Bison Ranch. I quickly explained what had happened yesterday and why we needed another figurine to replace the broken glass buffalo. I told Jack I heard Albert's mother say she was taking him for a train ride. Then I asked him where that was.

Jack properly introduced himself again and, this time, asked me what my name was. While he was doing so, I could hear something approaching us in the grass. I jumped up, thinking it was Mishka. Hoping he had managed to get away, I called out his name. To my surprise, it was the other rabbits that had gathered yesterday around the staircase and the two squirrels, and Sally, the little bird.

Jack's friends were asking what had taken him so long to get here; they had all left earlier in the day on different buggies and had been waiting all day for him to show up. They were eager to start the Jack-a-Lope Festival when Jack said, "Wait! You haven't heard all of it! I must warn you of the one they call Albert and his mother, who are here at the Ranch this very day!" He lowered his voice when he told how Albert and his mother discovered us hiding under the seat in the buggy.

Pointing to me, he said, "Albert's mother still has his little brother Mishka. They would have had me to, except I was able to hide." Then pointing towards the gift shop, he said. "That lady has brainwashed Mishka and is holding him captive in her coat."

Shocked, Jack's friends took a step backward; Jack walked over and stood by me; he was trying not to laugh as his face became more serious. He recalled how Albert had tortured me, and I became his play toy. Some of the rabbits thumped their hind feet in defiance of such a thing. Jack asked, "Who among us is brave enough to help get Mishka back?" Circling around his friends, he continued to beckon for their help; he asked them, "Are we just going to let these humans take us at will? Are we just play-toys for children? Are we going to allow Albert's mother to brainwash us?"

All the rabbits started looking at one another, thumping their feet, agreeing with Jack. Jack's voice became louder as he said, "First, it's a brother, then a sister; who knows when it could be you? I watched helplessly as Albert's mother hypnotized Mishka with her fingers simply by stroking him under his chin. Then she forced him into her coat and took him away!" Jack threw his front paw out in front of himself, clenched it into a fist, and asked, "Who's with me? Who is worthy of the length of their ears?" One by one, the rabbits and the squirrels piled their paws on top of Jack's paw.

It really surprised me that they were going to help. Jack sent a couple of the rabbits and Sally to look in the gift shop to check on Mishka. Then he whispered something to the squirrels, and they scurried away.

Jack's friends returned and reported that Mishka was still with Albert and his mother. They said Albert and his mother left the gift shop, heading toward the train for the tour around the ranch, and Mishka was still asleep in her coat. Sally stayed behind to keep an eye on him; that's when I noticed that the squirrels were nowhere to be seen; they had not returned with the rabbits.

We could hear a loud whistle blowing in the distance. Jack stood up, looking above the tall grass, announcing, "Come quick, the tour is starting."

Everyone raced through the grass, and barely able to keep up, I followed. We came upon a small building where many people waited for the train. Jack told me to stay close, and I followed him around the building's backside; we were going to hide under the stairs that passengers used to enter the train. I stopped for a moment to search the crowd to see if I could locate Mishka; just then, I heard another whistle and saw the train coming. Jack had already crossed over the tracks and yelled for me to jump to the other side where he was. With one giant leap, I made it! Jack and I crouched under the stairs as the train came to a stop. We watched as the passengers boarded to find their seats, starting to worry because I hadn't seen Albert or his mother.

Suddenly I heard the unwelcome squeal of Albert's voice as he screeched, "I want a train; I want one to play with at home!" Ignoring his demands, Albert's mother said, "Come, Albert, and don't drop your ice cream." They walked to the back of the rail car and took a seat; Jack pointed to me and then to the rear entrance. Indicating it was leaving, the train whistled again.

Quickly we ran for the door. Jack was yelling for me to hurry; I ran as fast as I could. The train was picking up speed. I jumped for the step and missed. Still running to keep up with the train, I noticed

Albert's mother was holding my brother. I called out to Mishka, and he popped his head out of her coat. Jack ran alongside me, yelling, "Jump now, Manny!" I jumped with all my might; I had made it. I was on the train with Mishka. Quickly I looked to see if Jack had jumped with me; I saw he was still running beside the train. Then he stopped and pointed; he was trying to tell me something when I heard a squeal; it was Albert. I had landed in the seat next to him. He grabbed me and held me up to the window. I watched as Jack disappeared in the distance.

I struggled to get free, but Albert had a good hold on me. He jumped to his feet, swinging me in his mother's direction, and announced proudly, "Look who has missed me and has come back!" Then he jumped up and down and squeezed me so tight to his chest that I gasped for air while he chanted, "Mine, mine, mine, it's my kitty."

Mishka popped his head out of Albert's mother's coat again, yawned, then said, "Will you stop playing with that kid."

Albert's mother told him to sit down because the train was moving. She told him to get ready to see the camels. Albert squealed again and threw himself down in his seat.

Mishka asked me, "So now that we are here, when should we pick up the figurine and head home. Maybe we could hang out for a while longer. I heard Albert's mother say they were spending the night in a cabin. That could be fun, Manny. Do you wanna stay?"

I started to say something to Mishka, but the train began to slow down so the passengers could see the camels. Albert jumped to his feet again and screamed, "I can't see. I wanna see the camels! Now!"

Albert's mother explained that he needed to stay in his seat so he wouldn't fall. He held me out the window so I could see the camels too. I felt terrified and began to struggle, afraid he was going to drop me, and I would get separated from Mishka again.

Finally, Albert's mother helped him to sit down, and he began to rub his sticky ice cream-coated hands on my head. I looked at Mishka, telling him he needed to pay attention to me so we could get away from Albert and his mother.

Mishka turned his head to look at the camels and said, "Paula is gone, and I think we should take in the sights and enjoy the freedom. We have plenty of time to get a new figurine to replace the one you broke, so just chill out!"

Albert started to play with my tail, and I had had enough, so I flexed my hind feet and dug my toenails into his leg. He stopped playing with my tail for a moment and looked at me, then gave it a tug.

Sinking every one of my claws into his leg, I swished my tail and jerked it away from Albert, then told Mishka that we were going home as soon as the ride was over. Rubbing his head against Albert's mother, Mishka muttered, "Okay, captain, no fun!"

Albert continued to scream his demands and wants; each time, the train slowed to look at the different animals. I searched for Jack and his friends, but they were nowhere to be found in the field. I wondered if they had started their Jack-a-Lope Festival.

The train made its way to the last animal. Once again, an excited and squealing Albert thrust me to the rail and held me out to see the buffalo. I was now face to face with an enormous beast. It sniffed me; Mishka jumped over Albert, put his feet on the rail, and marveled at its size. My brother looked back at me and said, "Hey, he looks just like the figurine you broke."

I growled and hissed, "Mishka, if you would learn to listen, we could have been home already."

That's when the buffalo said, "Mishka! It's you; you're the two cats, Manny, and Mishka! Jack was just here telling me about you! So, this must be *the* Albert and his evil mother!"

Mishka asked, "Who's Jack? Hey, how do you know about us?" Before the buffalo could answer, the train began to move and pulled away. Mishka threw a peace sign to the buffalo and said, "We'll be here all day!"

Albert's mother pulled Mishka from the rail and told Albert to sit down. My brother was curious now and started asking me questions. I tried to tell him about Jack and his friends when Albert decided to stuff me into his shirt. I resisted clawing at him because I knew the train ride was coming to an end. I could see that we were approaching the same little building from where we had left. I leaned over to tell Mishka that I wanted us to run once the train stopped, but Albert's mother wrapped him in her coat again and zipped it closed.

We exited the train and headed for a group of cabins. Albert started to complain, saying he wasn't done with the day. He wanted to play longer. His mother told him he needed a bath so they could get ready for dinner. A terrifying thought ran through my mind, Albert was sticky from the ice cream; I was sticky from his hands. Was I going to get a bath with sweet little Albert too?

The cabin we were in had two beds and a TV with a small bathroom. Albert's mother put Mishka on one of the beds and told Albert to get ready for his bath; instead, he ran to the window with me still under his arm. I could see horses standing near a stable; I wondered if Jack and his friends were there celebrating. Albert swung me around and around, holding me over his head. I felt like I would throw up, and he suddenly let go of me; thankfully, I landed on the bed beside Mishka.

Mishka jumped to the side, saying, "Wow, you really flew that time." He tried to give me a high five while asking me when we would have our dinner. Frustrated and upset, I grabbed him and said, "We are going home the first chance we get, now watch for the door to open."

I froze when I heard Albert's mother start the water for his bath. I felt weak and terrified, so I sat up to search the room for a place to hide.

Albert's mother came out of the bathroom, telling him to get ready for his bath. He reached for me, and I jumped. Albert chased me to the other side of the room. I ran under the table and jumped up in a chair. I could hear Albert squealing as he looked for me. Mishka rubbed at Albert's legs, but before Albert could pick him up, Albert's mother came into the room and led him away to his bath. Hearing the bathroom door close, I felt relieved.

Making sure Albert was gone, I peeked my head out from under the table, and Mishka jumped on me, yelling, "Found you!" Unable to help myself, I screamed in terror and clawed at the air.

My brother laughed and said, "It's only me; I thought we were playing hide-n-seek with your new best friend."

Quickly I jumped to the window, trying to claw my way out. Mishka jumped up beside me and started to claw the window with me. He said, "I don't understand this game; You'll have to explain it to me."

That's when Sally landed in the tree outside of our window. She was frantically trying to talk to us, only we couldn't hear her.

Mishka was surprised she was here and said, "Not this chattering little bird again; I can't understand a word it says."

Sally was pointing to the stables, and even though we couldn't hear her, I knew she was talking fast. I held my paw to my ear so she would know I couldn't hear her. Sally moved her wings, holding them to her head, indicating long ears; then, I knew she was talking about Jack and the other rabbits. She pointed to the stables again. Standing on my hind legs, I could see Jack and the others.

Jack was standing on the back of what appeared to be a giant, black-horned rabbit statue. He waved and motioned with his hands that he was on his way and not to worry. I waved back, wishing for the window to be open; I frantically started to claw at it again. Mishka stood beside me, looking to see who I was waving at, then noticed Jack and the others giving them the peace sign with a thumbs up.

Sally started to jump up and down and point behind us; it was Albert. He had finished his bath and was coming for me. I jumped in the air and ran to hide under the bed. Albert struggled to get under the bed after me; he reached for me when I heard his mother call out, "Come on, Albert, let's go have some pizza." He squealed and hurried out from under the bed.

I rushed to Mishka, asking him if he wanted to play follow-the-leader. Thinking if I made a game out of this, he would follow me. Just before the door opened, I ran between Albert's legs. Mishka chased me, whooping and hollering, thinking this was the best game in the world. So, I ran faster, dodging between Albert's legs again and then around his mother, who had just opened the door. I darted outside; once there, I yelled to Mishka but didn't hear anything. I felt afraid to look; turning, I saw Albert's mother stuffing him into her coat. I felt rage; I was tired of Albert and his mother. I ran in their direction, fully intending to get my brother back. Jack appeared before me, saying, "Wait, we will get him back." Then Albert and his mother disappeared.

Chapter 3

THE SUN WAS BEGINNING TO SET, AND I FELT EXHAUSTED. Jack led me to the stable where the annual Jack-a-Lope Festival was happening. Not only were Jack's friends there, but dozens of other rabbits from all over the country had shown up. Their celebration was in full swing; some were munching on carrots while others played slapjack. Stories of old and new could be heard throughout the stable.

Jack jumped onto the back of a giant, black-horned rabbit statue I had seen him standing on earlier. Everyone gathered around. He began to tell my story of Albert and his mother. The rabbits listened in terror as Jack recalled the torture I had endured at Albert's hands.

Gasps could be heard once Jack explained how Albert's mother hypnotized my brother and then held him captive in her coat. Jack worked himself up, beckoning their help; finally, he said, "Who's going to help get Mishka back? Who's with me?" But only Jack's friends responded. I could see the rest of the rabbits were afraid.

Jack slid down the side of the giant statue. He stood by the fire for a moment, and with pride, he encouraged his fellow rabbits by reciting the Jack-a-Lope legend. His story was one of bravery and sadness. Jack said, "Long ago, our ancestors were once as big as this stone statue. They roamed the land, free to come and go. Then humans came and used them as they pleased. They became slaves, used as work animals without regard for their well-being. Once they were no longer of this world, their pelts were stripped from their bodies and used as human clothes; their magnificent horns were also taken. Here on this very ground, my great, great grandfather, Jack Alan Lope, gave his life for all of the Jack-a-Lopes. He pleaded to the heavens for help, and the Gods listened, and with one swift move, he was turned to stone, but not before taking all the horns from every Jack-a-Lope and making their bodies smaller. They were safe now, no longer coveted, and could hide in the shadows, ensuring the survival of our kind."

Jack pointed to the stone statue again and said. "What the humans did to us is the very reason we are no longer called Jack-a-Lopes and why we are now known as rabbits. What will we be reduced to now if we don't get Mishka back?"

All the rabbits cheered, remembering the legends and stories they were told at bedtime when they were young. They stood in unison, ready to do anything necessary to help get Mishka back. Jack looked to see if I was listening; he motioned for me to join him by the fire. He told me he had sent his two best diggers and chewers to punch a hole into Albert and his mother's room.

At that moment, one of the rabbits approached us and whispered in Jack's ear. Jack said, "Hey everyone, it's time; we're not going to let these humans keep any of our friends or us locked up ever again! Let's go get Mishka!"

I was confused about how we would get my brother back. Jack motioned for me to follow him, and we ran to the window of the cabin that I had escaped from earlier. Two rabbits worked feverishly to dig and gnaw a hole in the wall. Jack told me to squeeze through the hole into the cabin and wait until Albert and his mother returned, then grab Mishka and come back through the hole. I tried to fit into the opening, but it wasn't big enough yet; as I pulled my head back, Jack said, "Don't worry."

He assured me he had a backup plan. He took me around to the front of the cabin and told me to wait for Albert and his mother to return. "When they open the door, run in and hide. We will signal you once the hole is completed, but wait until they are asleep before you try to escape." Jack said. "We will be right outside the window if you need us." Then he ran away, leaving me to hide outside the cabin door.

I started to drift off to sleep when I heard Albert and his mother approaching the cabin. He sounded a little afraid and was walking right beside his mother. Albert was full of questions tonight.

"Is it true what that man said? If I don't sit still, the giant Jack-a-Lope statue will get me in my bed tonight? Is there really a giant stone statue of a Jack-a-Lope?" Albert asked in a meek, frightened voice.

"No, Albert," his mother said, "the story you heard is only a tall tale. There are no such things as Jack-a-Lopes. Nothing is going to get you in your bed tonight."

Whispering, Albert repeated to his mother what the man sitting beside him in the restaurant said during dinner, "That big Jack-a-Lope that's here eats squealing children."

Then Albert's mother searched her pocket for the key to the door; she told Albert he could watch cartoons before going to bed.

The door opened, and I was unseen as I dashed into the cabin. I hid under the bed closest to the window. I watched as Albert's mother removed Mishka from her coat and placed him on the bed. He curled up in the pillows and went back to sleep. Albert came running from the bathroom in his pajamas with toothpaste all over his face. He jumped up and down on the bed, squealing for his mother to hurry up with the TV. His mother said, "Get in bed, Albert; it's been a long day."

Albert drove under the covers to watch TV, then suddenly sat up and said, "What is that noise? Is that a Jack-a-Lope coming to get me?"

Albert's mother sat up in her bed and listened; she told him again there was no such thing as Jack-a-Lopes. Albert insisted he could hear noises and pulled the covers over his head.

The rabbits were still working on the wall, and that's what Albert was hearing. I lay there under the bed listening to Albert squeal with delight as the cartoons played. Eventually, he was quiet, and the bed had finally stopped moving. I wondered if Albert had gone to sleep; peeking out from under the bed, I could see that Mishka and Albert's mother were asleep. Hoping that dear sweet Albert had drifted off as well, I peeked over the side, and to my relief, he was asleep. I jumped to the bed where Mishka was and landed on Albert's mother's hand; she jerked and began talking in her sleep as she rolled over. I froze mid-step and held my breath; afraid I would wake her. She went back to sleep. Just as I started to wake Mishka, Albert squealed, "My Kitty!"

I shook Mishka, frantically trying to wake him so we could leave. Albert bailed out of his bed and ran at me, screaming, "Mine, mine, mine!"

Albert and The Glass Figurine

I jumped to the floor and ran to the hole in the wall. I discovered the gap was still too small, and we were trapped in the room. Albert was close at my heels as I jumped to the windowsill; he reached to catch me but missed. Outside the window, I caught a glimpse of Jack and the other rabbits; they were still working on the hole.

Mishka sat up at the same time I jumped toward the bed. I missed the bed, landing on the nightstand and knocking the lamp over. The lights went out; it was pitch black in the room. Screaming, Albert ran in the direction of his mother's bed. Outside I could hear Jack calling to us. I struggled in the dark to find Mishka, calling out to him, then I felt someone pick me up, it was Albert, and then his mother bellowed, "What is going on in here?" All I could hear at this point was rustling in the room, then the lights came back on, and there stood Jack and the other rabbits.

They were lined up on Albert's bed, dusty and covered in debris. Giving them the appearance of tiny horns. Albert's mother gasped in disbelief at Jack and his friends. She reached for my brother and then Albert's hand. Jack said in a loud voice, "No more will they take us at will. Get-em!"

Jack and his friends started running around the room, causing a commotion. Albert was screaming and climbed up the front of his mother, knocking her to the floor. The rabbits raced around and over the top of them. At the top of his lungs, Albert promised to be good and sit still, begging them not to get him. Jack signaled to me to grab Mishka and leave. We waited for Jack and the others by the stables, the sun was rising, and it was going to be a great day. I thanked Jack for helping me. Mishka asked how we were going to get home. Jack said a bus would be leaving very soon.

Finally, the bus arrived, and we waved goodbye to our new friends; I had a death grip on my brother's tail as we headed back to town. Mishka was full of questions, and I told him we would talk about it when we got home.

Soon the bus pulled into the empty parking lot where we had boarded the buggies the day before. Mishka was eager to get home; he wanted a snack. He asked me what we should do about the broken figurine. I told him it didn't matter anymore. I was just thankful we were together and home again. We would face the music together when Paula came home.

As we approached the front steps, Mishka spied the squirrels; they were standing in front of our porch. My brother crouched down, preparing to pounce on them. He whispered, asking, "Who do they think they are?"

I held Mishka's tail tighter, holding him back. The squirrels laughed and held up a brand-new glass buffalo figurine. Then they sat it on the porch steps and scurried away. My brother looked from me to the glass figurine; he was confused. Grabbing the figurine, I pushed Mishka into the house. Breathing a massive sigh of relief, I closed the door. We made it home, and I was never so happy to be here.

I went to the living room and placed the glass buffalo figurine next to Paula's lamp. The phone rang; we listened to the caller; it was a female's voice. It said, "Hi Paula, it's just me, Brenda. I hope you are enjoying your vacation. Albert and I just got home from spending the night at the Bison Ranch. You are never going to believe what happened. You'll never guess who is on the newspaper's front page this morning. It's a picture of Albert and me. Albert is holding a cute little gray kitty. I'll tell you about it over breakfast at the Elks Lodge when you get home."

THE END

Elizabeth James

Elizabeth James
Purebred Red Female Dachshund
Born: August 1, 2019

I enjoy playing with toys, digging in the yard, barking, and chasing the neighbor's cat. Favorite indoor past times include but are not limited to racing through the house, greeting guests at the door, collecting items that are not mine, and hiding them in my bed. I seriously cannot imagine a life without my Mom, and my sister and brother.

Playtime is a particularly special time for me. It's where I do my most important work with my toys. I'm currently considering creating a series of video tutorials on proper squeaker removal. My brother tells me that if I listen to his suggestions and give him my treats, these video tutorials could win massively in a Drama Series. However, I'm not sure if my brother is referring to my treats or the videos.

Sager Jane

Sager Jane
Sable Female Chihuahua/Dachshund
(Also known as a Chiweenie)
Born: August 31, 2013

I enjoy playing with toys and pretending that I'm a cattle dog herding cows down a dusty trail. Snapping at every heel from here to the horizon. My Aunt Goldie can personally attest to my swiftness and accuracy.

I am also proficient at getting on the dining room table. I can have a quick bite of food and return to the floor without anyone ever having been aware that I've done so!

My favorite thing ever is to keep my sister and brother from getting into trouble, and I don't care if they think I am a fun sucker! I love to be in charge.

Mr. Wienie
Purebred Black & Tan Male Dachshund
Born: February 2, 2011

I enjoy all things food and being in Grandma's room. She and I spend most days watching television and sharing her snacks, especially when she doesn't know it. I am most passionate about defending the fence line in the yard!

Anytime delivery personnel arrive, I always ensure they are aware of our presence. I feel that this is of the utmost importance to a dachshund of my caliber.

So, back to snacks! Not just any snack will do! It must start and end with the word Bacon. There is no substitute. Because that's how I roll.

Pepper Ann
Black Bombay Female Feline
(Veterinarian Verified)
Born: April 1, 2022

I am Elizabeth, Sager, and Mr. Wienie's cousin. My Mom is Cendy J. Hatfield, but everyone calls her Madmouzzie. I enjoy playing with my stuffed toy, Puppy; I carry him all over the house.

My favorite late-night activities include but are not limited to singing the song of my people, hiding my Dad's socks, and offering massages while my Mother is trying to sleep. The best and most fun thing of all in the middle of the night is pretending I'm a race car driver in the Indy 500 and my parent's bed is the race track.

I'm still just a kitten trying to learn the ways of a Savage. I want to be just like my cousins. My Mom tells me that soon I will be written into some of her stories. How exciting is that?

Wendy J. Hatfield has found herself fortunate enough these days to spend each day doing exactly as she pleases. Throughout her life, she has never known the meaning of the word quit.

She experienced her share of typical growing pains and everything that went with it. She found everlasting love and lived twenty-nine glorious years of marriage to then be faced with the devastating loss of her husband.

The survivor in Wendy pulled up her bootstraps and went back to the retail workforce as the CEM of Operations for a world-known craft house in her location for 10 years.

She is an identical mirror image twin to Cendy J. Hatfield. She is a celebrated author who is currently retired and enjoys traveling. Her greatest pleasures are spending time with her family and playing with, photographing, and writing about her three beautiful dachshunds, Elizabeth James, Sager Jane, and Mr. Wienie.

Cendy and her Husband Tom

Cendy J. Hatfield is the identical mirror image twin to Wendy J. Hatfield. Cendy, like her twin Wendy, she is also a celebrated author. She is also known on social media for her famous nom de plume, Madmouzzie.

Cendy is literally the driving force behind most of the stories posted as "The Diner" featured on Elizabeth and The Savages UnChained FaceBook page. The Diner posts are about the daily antics of Elizabeth James, Sager Jane, Mr. Wienie, and their friends.

She enjoys traveling with her husband, Tom. Their greatest pleasure is spending time together with family and riding their Harley-Davidson Motorcycle. What more can be said here. Life is Good!

A special thanks to the fans of Elizabeth and The Savages Unchained on all our social media.

Your love and encouragement toward Elizabeth and the Savages' daily activity and antics helped make all of this possible.

**Read on for an excerpt from
Cendy J. Hatfield's upcoming Trilogy About Lottie**

Lottie aka Sager Jane

Sager had met a Scottish terrier named Archie, who wore a bowler hat and a bow tie. She had left instructions for Mr. Wienie to sit with Elizabeth while she had a candle-lit dinner with Archie on the beach that night.

The last night we spent in Corpus Christi was torture for Elizabeth. She was torn between wanting to stay forever in Texas and missing home. Elizabeth helped Sager wiggle into a relatively tight red dress. Then Elizabeth smoothed Sager's hair down. "It's fun to visit the carnival. But who wants to live there?" Sager said to Elizabeth. Elizabeth smiled and then hugged her.

Archie knocked on the door; Sager yelled down the hallway for Mr. Wienie to let Archie in and tell him she would be there in a minute. When Sager entered the room, she found Archie lying on the floor with his bag next to him; his bow tie was askew. Mr. Wienie had his feet on Archie's chest, his hat in his mouth, growling and demanding to know if Archie was a spy? "Wienie," Sager yelled. When Mr. Wienie wouldn't let Archie up. She nipped his tail and told him to sit down.

As Mr. Wienie sat down, he said, "Sager, how do we know this guy isn't a spy? The only thing I trust about him right now is that he smells like food." Glaring at Archie, Mr. Wienie said, "Are we sure you're not a spy, Archie? Who wears aftershave that smells like oatmeal and carrots?"

Sager snatched Archie's bowler hat away from Mr. Wienie. "We're going out for dinner now, and then Archie is taking me to the carnival," Sager told Wienie and Elizabeth. "You two need to stay in the room tonight. I have my cell phone should you need me. Elizabeth, you need to look after our brother; I think he's had too much sun. You can order room service should you get hungry." Sager said to Elizabeth as she kissed her sister on the forehead.

Mr. Wienie and Elizabeth watched as Archie bowed to Sager before extending his arm to escort her from the room. Elizabeth raced to the door; she opened it just enough to witness her sister giggling and kissing Archie.

Mr. Wienie turned on the tv and asked Elizabeth what she wanted to watch; she spun away from the door, closing it, telling Mr. Wienie what she had just seen their sister do. It was precisely what Mr. Wienie needed to hear; he was confident that Archie was a spy. Leaping from the sofa, he told Elizabeth to get his flip-flops and a flashlight.

"Hurry up, Elizabeth! It's dark outside. No one gives two figs what your hair looks like." Mr. Wienie impatiently said, waiting at the door to their room. "Did Sager say which restaurant they would be dining at tonight on the beach?"

"Wienie, I'm not fixing my hair; I'm putting disguises together for us. Sager told us to stay in the room; if she finds out we followed her, our sister will have both our heads." Putting the stuff she gathered in front of Mr. Wienie, Elizabeth said, "Can you believe Sager is out on a date? Oh, and I can't believe she actually giggled."

It took some time for Elizabeth to squeeze Wienie into a bathrobe that she found behind the bathroom door. She added a shower cap stuffed with pink curlers. As she clipped it to Mr. Wienie's head, she arranged some curlers so they would stick out. Next, Elizabeth tied a purple silk scarf around Mr. Wienie's neck, then added lipstick. Finally, she had Mr. Wienie step into the new pair of high heels she had bought that day. Elizabeth covered her mouth and giggled from behind her paws as she watched Mr. Wienie teetering back and forth, trying to make his way to the full-length mirror that stood across the room next to the door. When Mr. Wienie saw himself in the mirror, he said, "Really, Elizabeth! I look like an old lady! I look like our neighbor Mrs. Jackson."

While Elizabeth dressed in a black outfit with a matching mask and black boots, Mr. Wienie turned from side to side to look at himself in the mirror. "Why do I have to wear this robe that makes me look fat, and you get to look like a cool bat dog on a heist?" Mr. Wienie asked as he practiced walking in Elizabeth's high heels.

Elizabeth tried not to giggle at Mr. Wienie as she told him, "I grabbed a backpack to carry the things we might need. With these disguises, Sager will never suspect it's us. We've got one flashlight, a rope, and binoculars."

"Okay, okay, let's go, Elizabeth. I don't like the smell of Archie. Who wears oatmeal and carrot aftershave? What has gotten into Sager's head? She never trusts anyone. Mom is right people do strange things when they're on vacation. Traveling and dating? Who ever heard of such a thing? Elizabeth, did you throw some bacon in that bag? I'm hungry." Mr. Wienie said as they made their way out of their room and down the hallway to the elevator.

Mr. Wienie and Elizabeth made it out of the hotel and down the back stairs to a walkway leading to another set of stairs that led directly to the beach. Mr. Wienie asked Elizabeth for the binoculars. He scanned the beach and the many candlelit tables. About halfway down the beach, he finally found Sager and Archie's table. Mr. Wienie gasped when he saw Archie get out of his chair and down on one knee.

The Scottish terrier dug through his bag and held up a box. Sager swooned as she took a neckless from the box and put it around her neck. Archie leaped to his feet and kissed Sager on the cheek. Mr. Wienie growled and gave the binoculars back to Elizabeth, saying, "Let's move out, Elizabeth." Then he lifted his robe a little higher and started down the stairs toward the sandy beach.

"What makes you think Archie is a spy Wienie?" Elizabeth asked. Then followed Mr. Wienie down the stairs; she stopped every now and then to hide behind the poles of the staircase. She would lean out, looking both ways; then, she would slink to the next pole. She was quietly humming her own 'Mission Impossible' tune the whole time.

"Elizabeth, what are you doing?" Mr. Wienie said as the robe he was wearing caught the heel of his shoe. "Stop playing, Elizabeth; this is serious." He said as he adjusted the shower cap on his head yet again. "You're drawing attention to us."

While Mr. Wienie and Elizabeth waited in line for their turn to get a table. Elizabeth stood with the binoculars, watching Sager and Archie. She could see Sager holding Archie's bag in her lap. She would lean down and laugh into the bag every now and then. It was strange to watch. "Mr. Wienie, why would Sager laugh into Archie's bag?"

Mr. Wienie took the binoculars to see for himself and noticed Sager was eating fish and chips. After he told Elizabeth what Sager was eating, she said, "Sager hates fish. What has gotten into our sister? She is acting completely different."

When Elizabeth and Mr. Wienie's turn came to be seated, in a high-pitched voice, Mr. Wienie told the waiter they wanted a table by the ocean. The waiter took them to a table just behind Sager and Archie. As Elizabeth and Mr. Wienie were looking at the menu, Sager got up from her table, walked past them, and headed to the ladies' room. Elizabeth ducked behind her menu; Mr. Wienie wasn't fast enough. Sager smiled at Mr. Wienie and said, "Oh, madame, what a beautiful scarf. I have one just like it."

"Why, thank you, sweet child. I'm from Georgia, where the scarfs are made from peach fuzz." Mr. Wienie said in his high-pitched voice.

Sager paused, looking back over her shoulder. Elizabeth kicked Mr. Wienie under the table, startled; he picked up the water glass in front of him; taking a long drink, he smeared lipstick up the side of his face.

The waiter was still waiting for Elizabeth and Mr. Wienie to place an order. Elizabeth told the waiter to bring them two number sevens without even looking at the menu. Then she grabbed her brother's paw and told Sager, "My momma is from the old country." Sager waved, telling them to have a pleasant evening, and continued to make her way to the ladies' room.

Archie's phone rang as the waiter brought Mr. Wienie and Elizabeth their number seven dinners. While Elizabeth was trying to remind Mr. Wienie that they were supposed to be Mrs. Jackson and her daughter from the old country, Mr. Wienie climbed on top of the table, trying to better hear Archie's conversation.

"Wienie! You're standing on the table and drawing attention to us again." Elizabeth said, trying to push him back into his chair.

"It's fine, Elizabeth. Look, I'm eating my dinner." Mr. Wienie said as he spooned a mouth full of his number seven dinner into his mouth. He chewed the food and promptly spit it on the tablecloth. Coughing, Mr. Wienie dug at his mouth, saying, "What in the world is that?"

"Seaweed cakes," Elizabeth answered. She wasn't happy about the thought of eating seaweed either. Elizabeth had only ordered the number seven because every restaurant she had been in always had a number seven bacon burger.

Still wiping his mouth, Mr. Wienie said, "Well, that sure could use some…." Unbeknownst to Mr. Wienie, Sager was standing directly behind him. "Bacon! Or is that not how they serve it in the old country?" Sager snapped, then she smiled and smacked Mr. Wienie on the butt. "Get off that table, Mrs. Jackson! Take your daughter home, and then come back here." Sager said, and then she smiled and kissed Elizabeth on the top of the head. She whispered good night, then continued to her table, where Archie was still on the phone. As Elizabeth helped Mr. Wienie climb off the table, she noticed Sager had a key on a chain around her neck. She wanted to ask Sager if it was a present from Archie, but she knew they were in trouble for following their sister, so she didn't. When Mr. Wienie and Elizabeth returned to their room, she asked him about the necklace Sager had around her neck. Mr. Wienie explained that through the binoculars, he had seen Archie get down on one knee and propose marriage to their sister. Elizabeth gasped, saying, "Wienie, she must have said yes."

Coming Soon in Hardcover

OUR SOCIAL MEDIA

Facebook
Elizabeth and The Savages UnChained

Instagram
@wendyandheroutlaws

YouTube
@asalwaysitsmewendy
@Madmouzzie

TikTok
@wendyandheroutlaws
@madmouzzie

Printed in the USA
CPSIA information can be obtained
at www.ICGtesting.com
LVHW041222140923
757946LV00003B/472

9 798823 005654